HERE'S **HEATHCLIFF** by Geo Gately

AMERICA'S
CRAZIEST
CAT!

Volume I

© McNaught Synd., Inc.

THE BEST OF SUNDAY WITH HEATHCLIFF

AND THE GOOD LIFE

TOR

A TOM DOHERTY ASSOCIATES BOOK

This is a work of fiction. All the characters and events portrayed in this book are fictional, and any resemblance to real people or incidents is purely coincidental.

HEATHCLIFF AND THE GOOD LIFE
Volume I of HERE'S HEATHCLIFF

Reprinted by arrangement with Windmill Books, Inc. and Simon and Schuster, a division of Gulf and Western Corp.

First Tor printing: December 1985

A TOR Book

Published by Tom Doherty Associates, Inc.
49 West 24 Street
New York, N.Y. 10010

ISBN: 0-812-56819-2
CAN. ED.: 0-812-56820-6

Printed in the United States of America

0 9 8 7 6 5 4

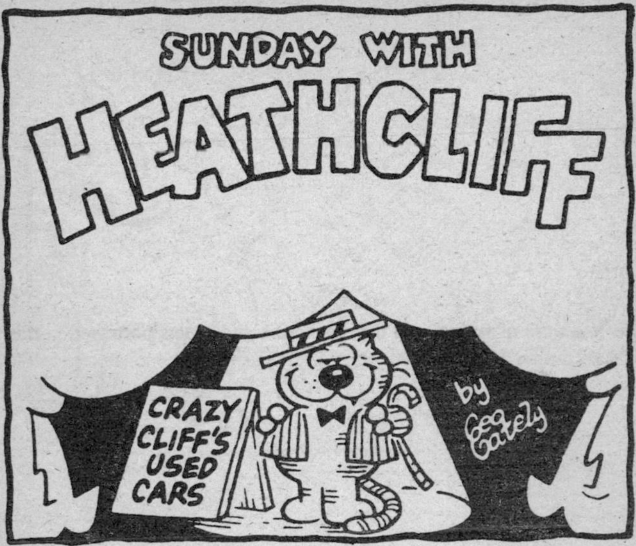
SUNDAY WITH
HEATHCLIFF
CRAZY CLIFF'S USED CARS
by Geo Gately

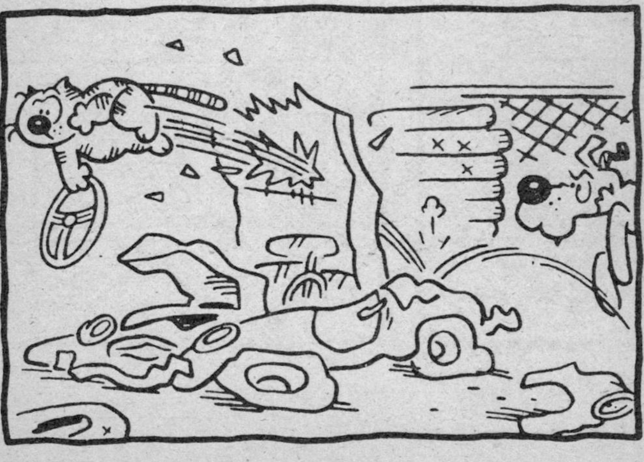

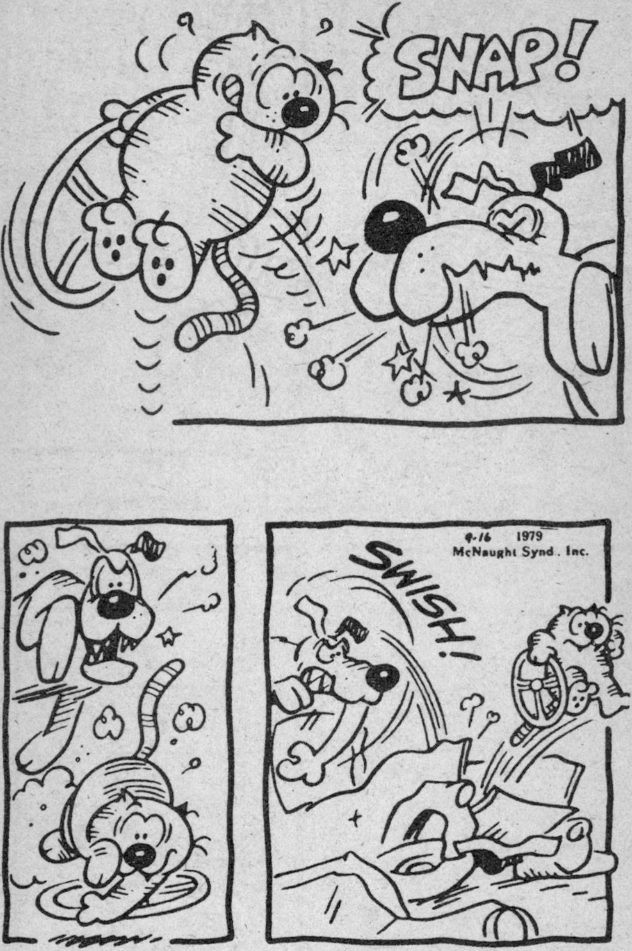
SNAP!
SWISH!
9-16 1979
McNaught Synd., Inc.

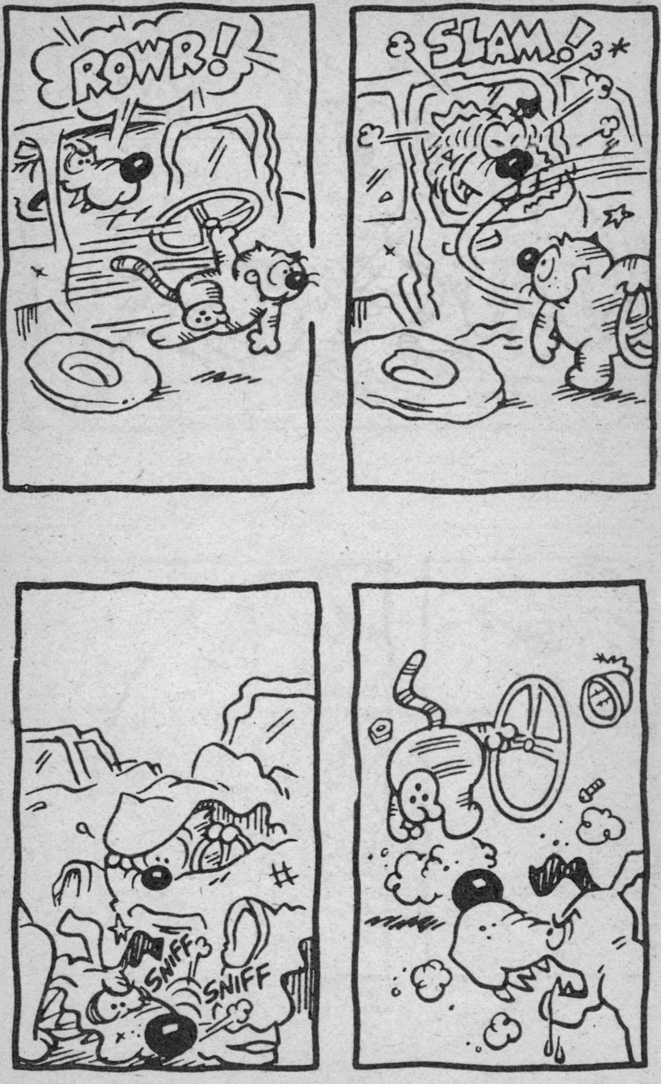
ROWR!
SLAM!
SNIFF
SNIFF

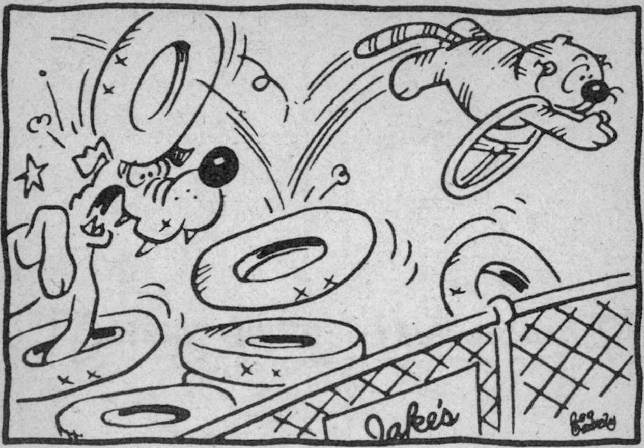
Jake's

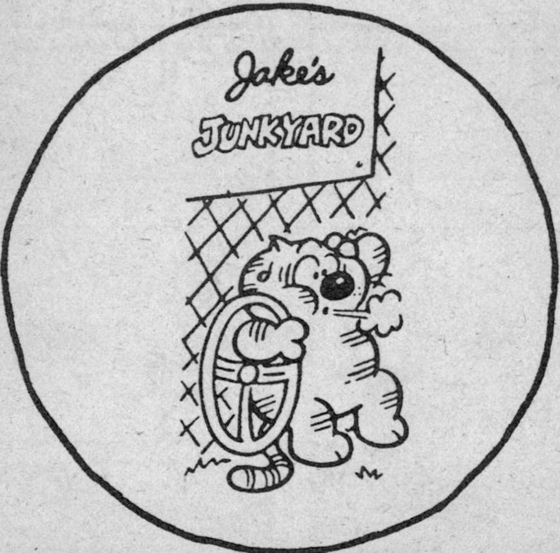
Jake's
JUNKYARD

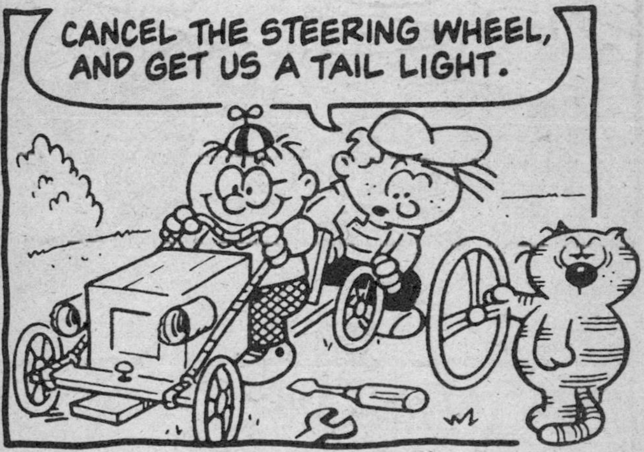
CANCEL THE STEERING WHEEL, AND GET US A TAIL LIGHT.

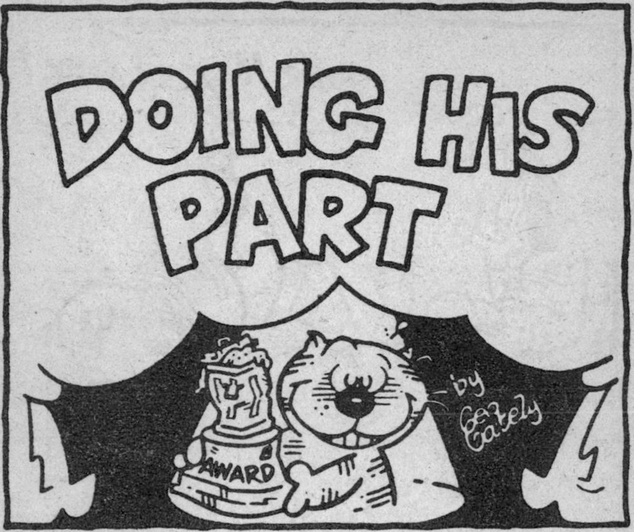
DOING HIS PART
AWARD
by

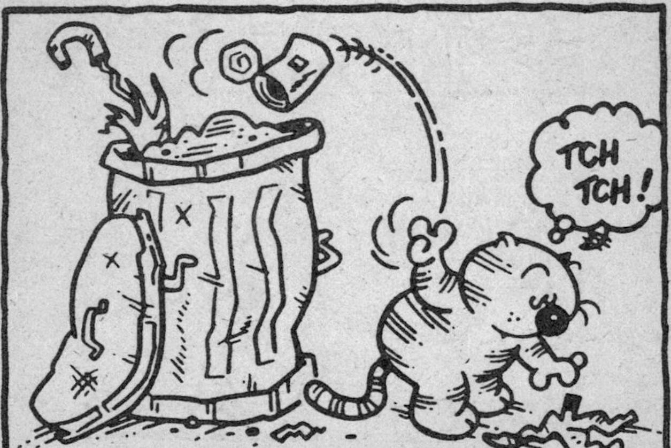
TCH TCH!

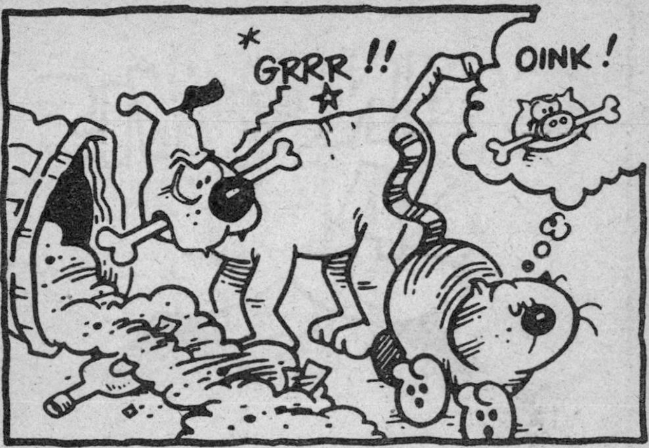
GRRR!!
OINK!

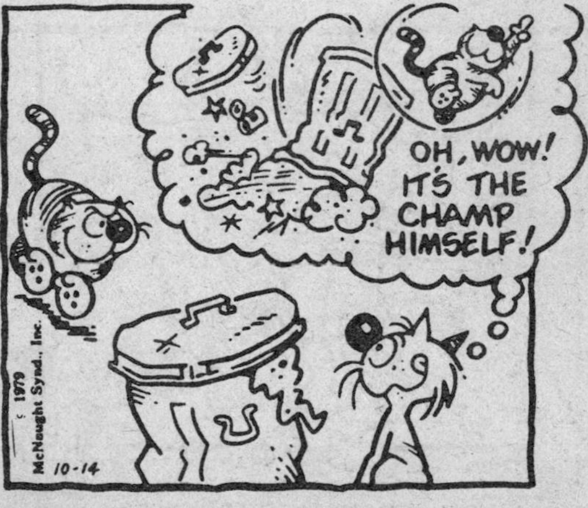
OH, WOW! IT'S THE CHAMP HIMSELF!
© 1979 McNaught Synd., Inc.
10-14

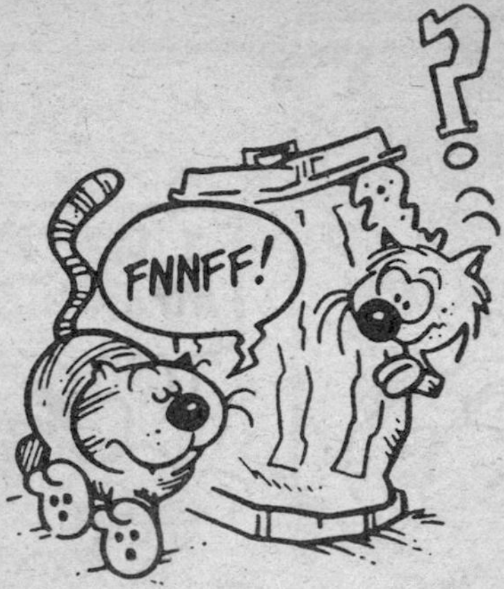
FNNFF!

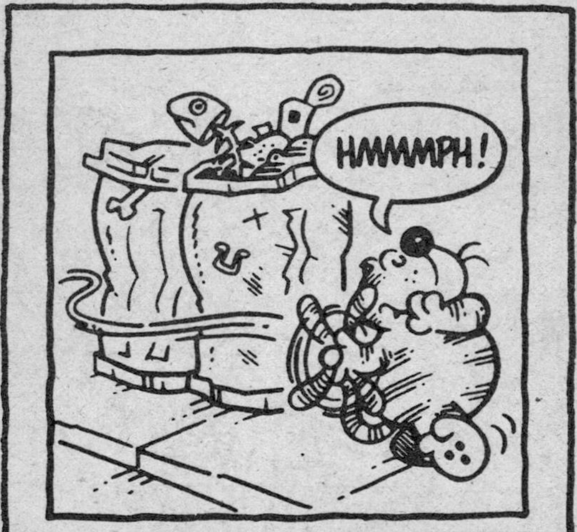
HMMMPH!

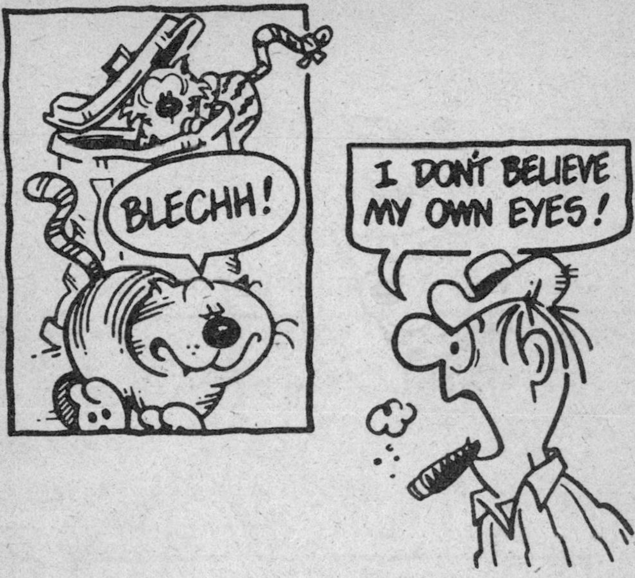
BLECHH!
I DON'T BELIEVE MY OWN EYES!

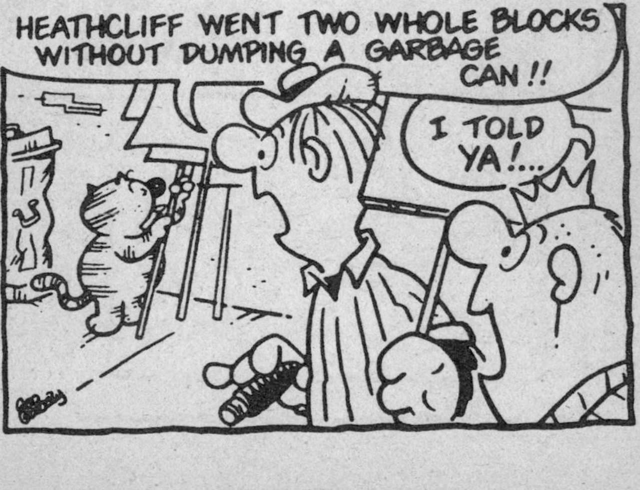
HEATHCLIFF WENT TWO WHOLE BLOCKS WITHOUT DUMPING A GARBAGE CAN!!
I TOLD YA!...

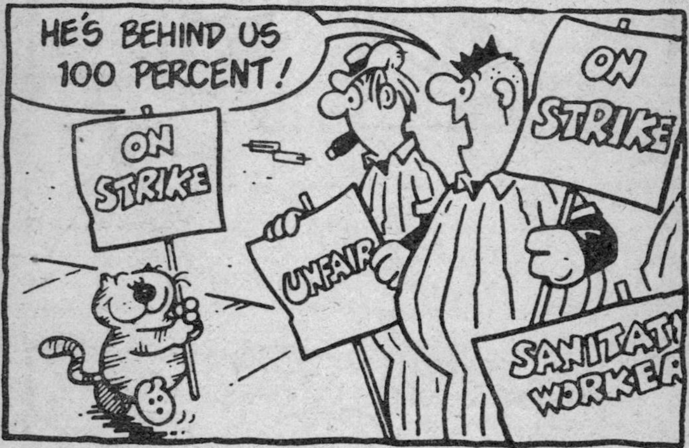
HE'S BEHIND US 100 PERCENT!
ON STRIKE
UNFAIR
ON STRIKE

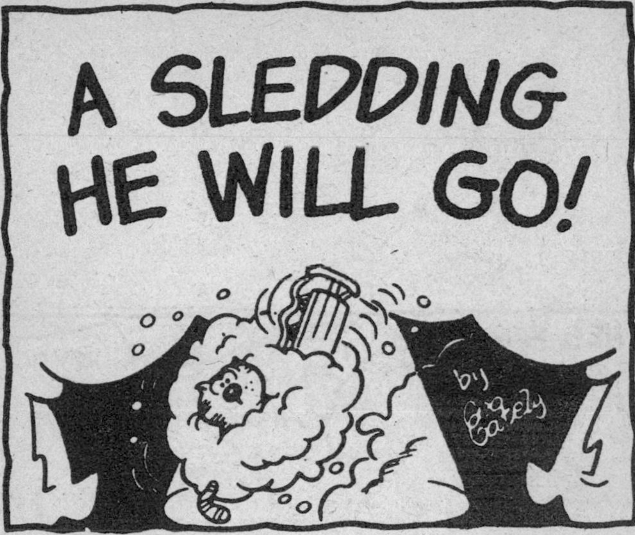
A SLEDDING HE WILL GO!

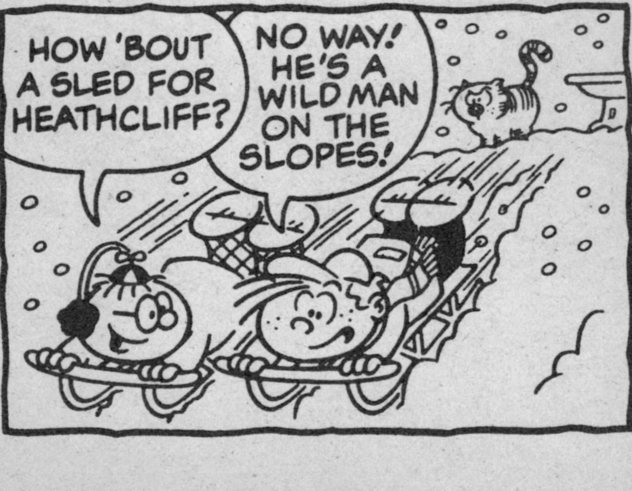
HOW 'BOUT A SLED FOR HEATHCLIFF?
NO WAY! HE'S A WILD MAN ON THE SLOPES!

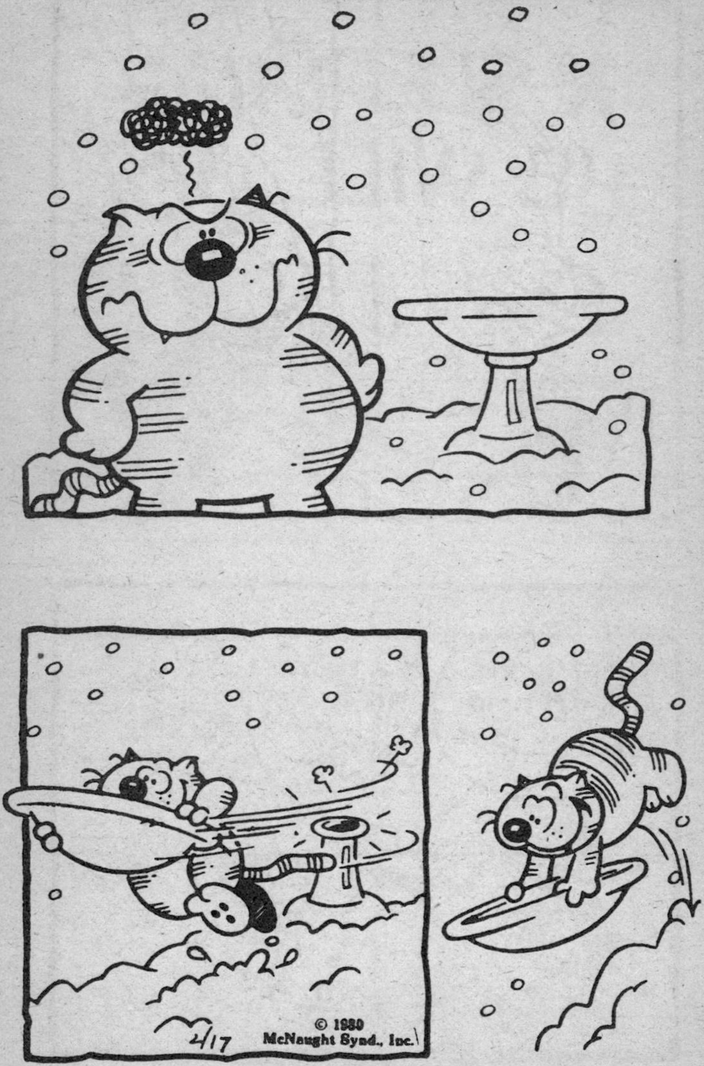

4/17
© 1980
McNaught Synd., Inc.

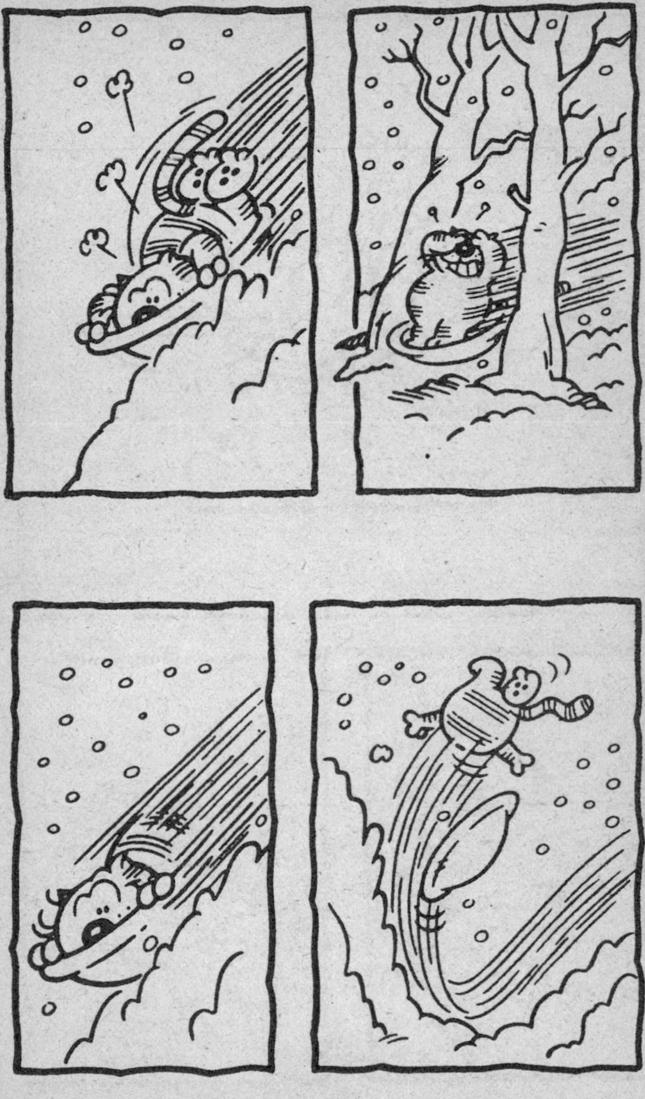

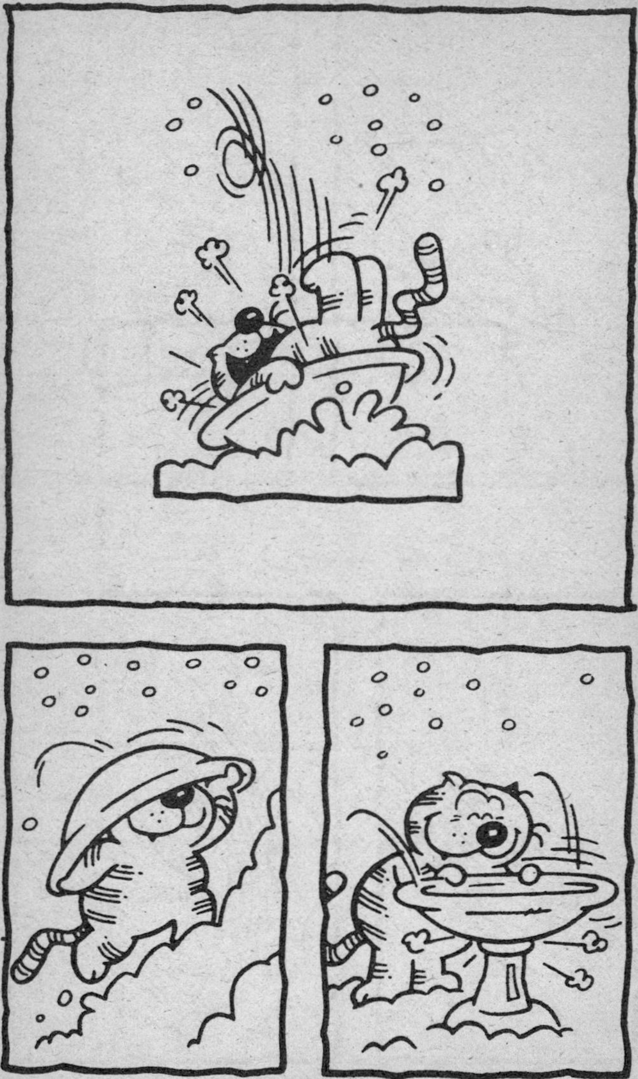

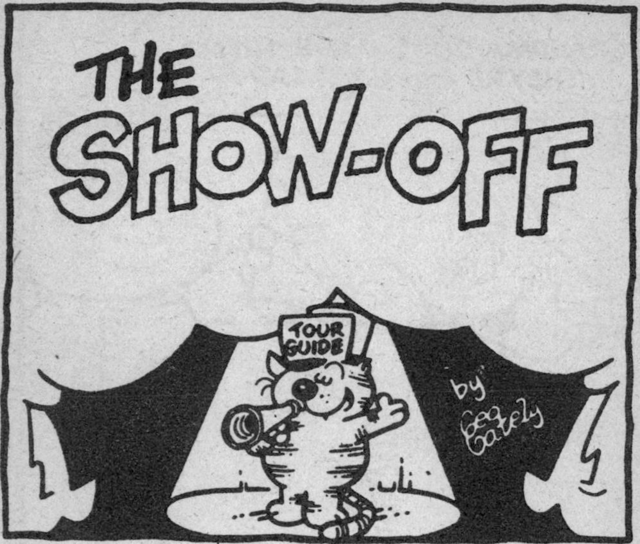
THE SHOW-OFF
TOUR GUIDE
by Greg Gately

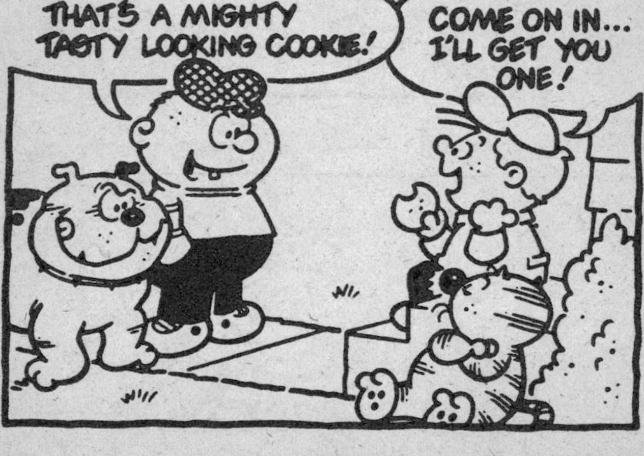
THAT'S A MIGHTY TASTY LOOKING COOKIE!
COME ON IN... I'LL GET YOU ONE!

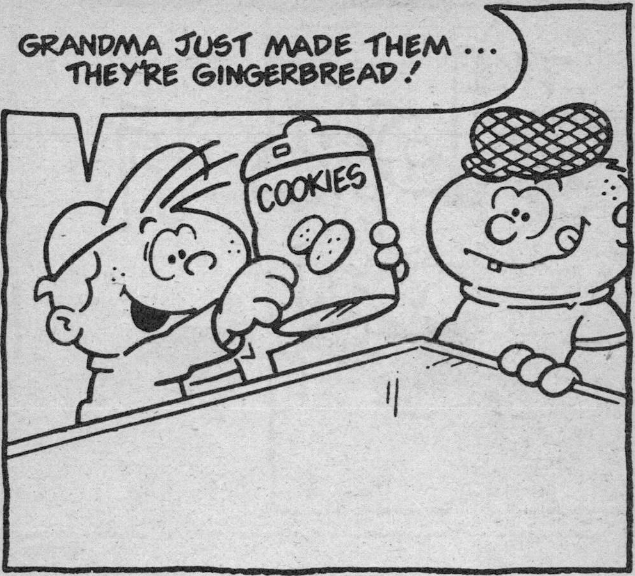
GRANDMA JUST MADE THEM ...
THEY'RE GINGERBREAD!
COOKIES

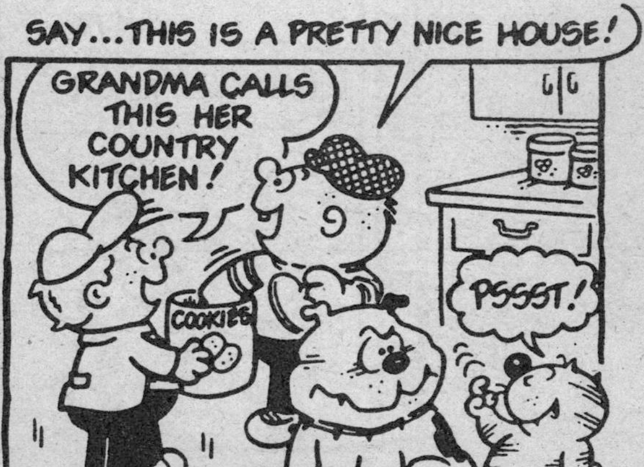
SAY...THIS IS A PRETTY NICE HOUSE!
GRANDMA CALLS THIS HER COUNTRY KITCHEN!
COOKIES
PSSST!

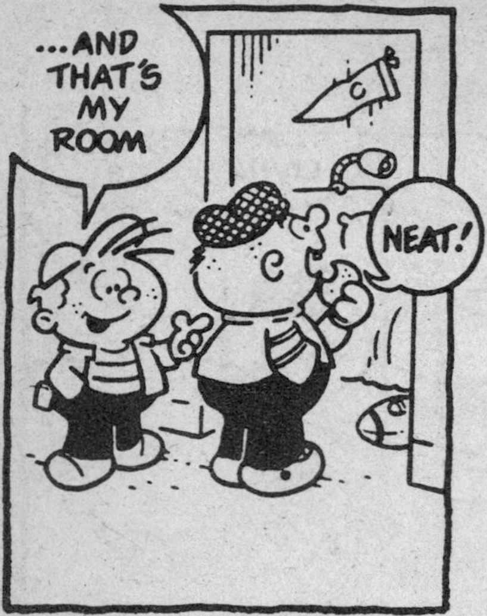
...AND THAT'S MY ROOM
NEAT!

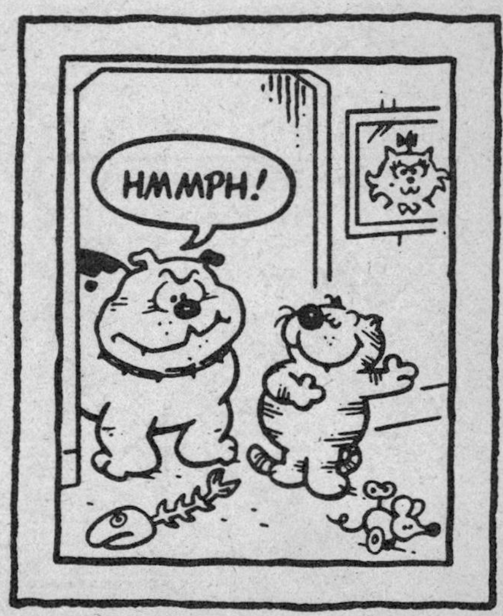
HMMPH!

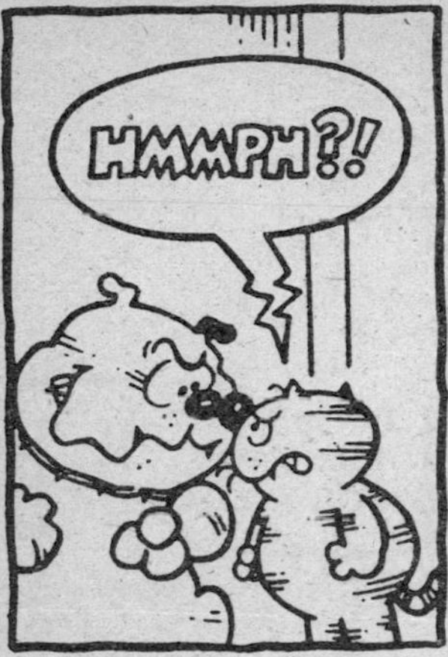
HMMPH?!

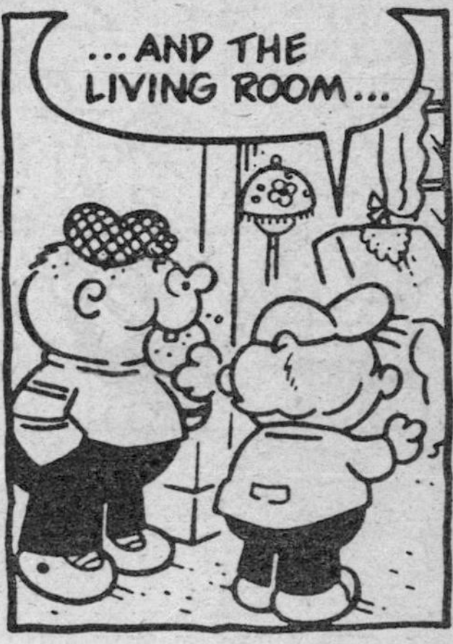
...AND THE LIVING ROOM...

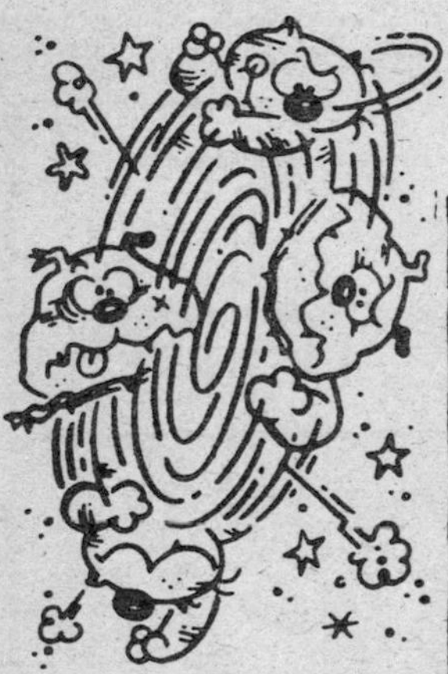

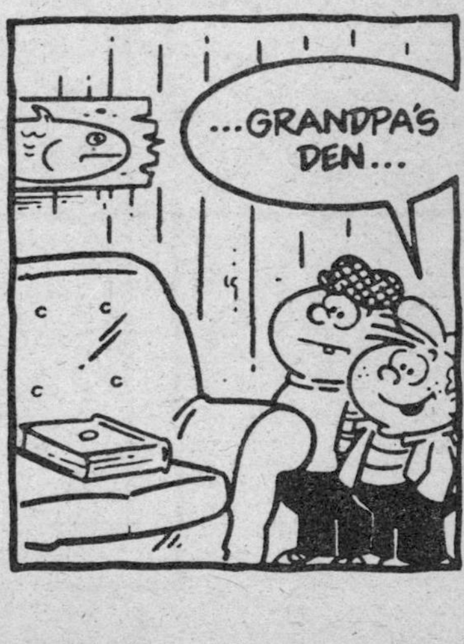
...GRANDPA'S DEN...

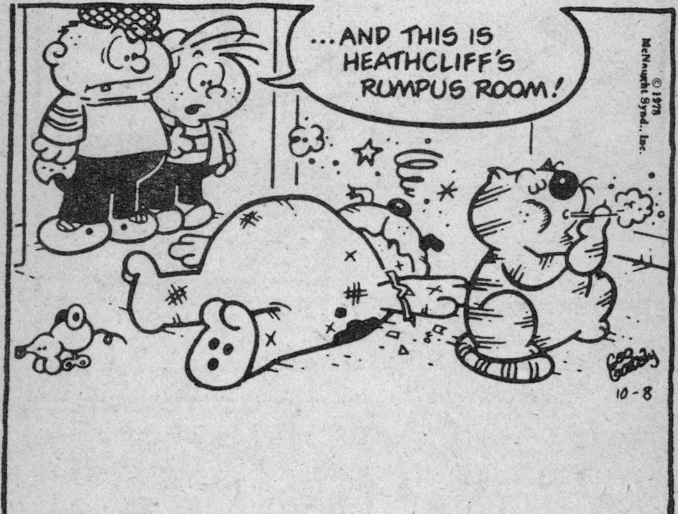

...AND THIS IS HEATHCLIFF'S RUMPUS ROOM!
© 1978 McNaught Synd., Inc.
10-8

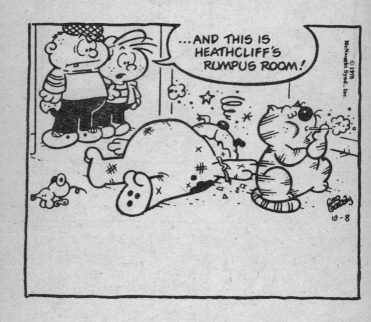

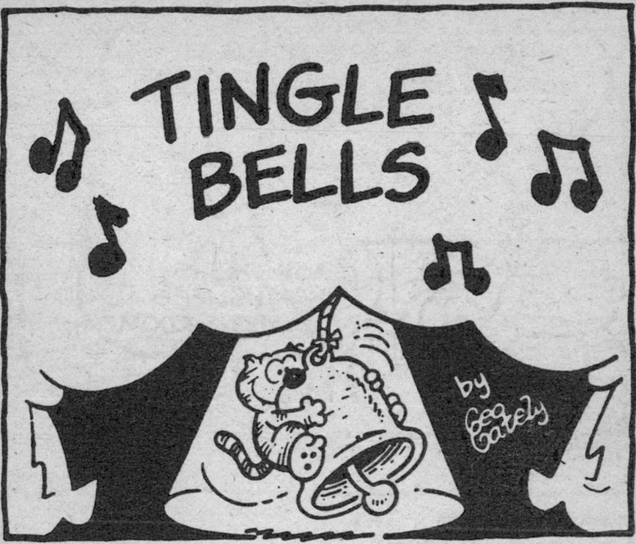
TINGLE BELLS
by Geo Gately

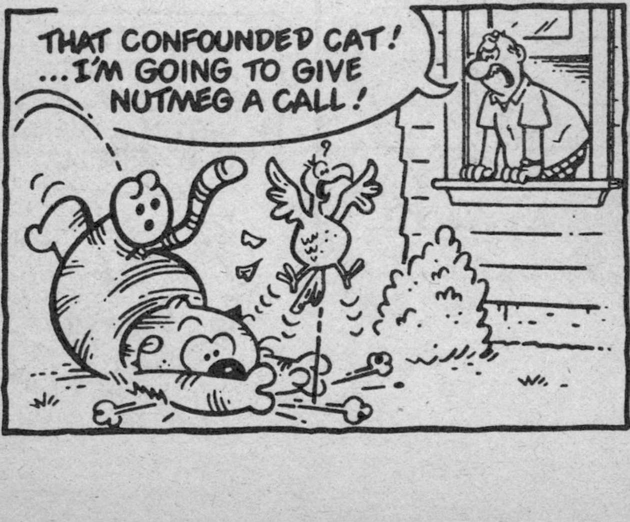
THAT CONFOUNDED CAT! ...I'M GOING TO GIVE NUTMEG A CALL!

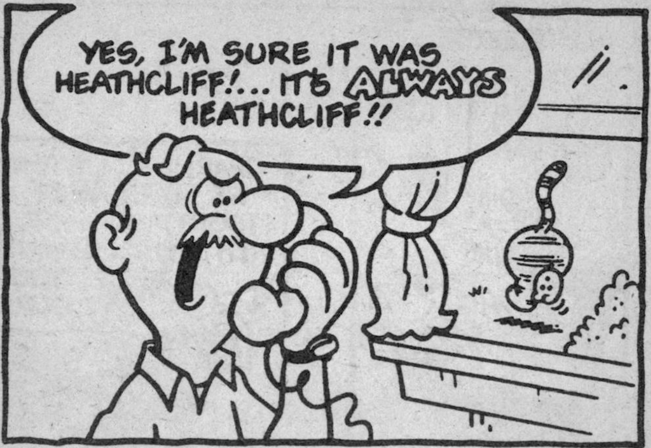
YES, I'M SURE IT WAS HEATHCLIFF!... IT'S ALWAYS HEATHCLIFF!!

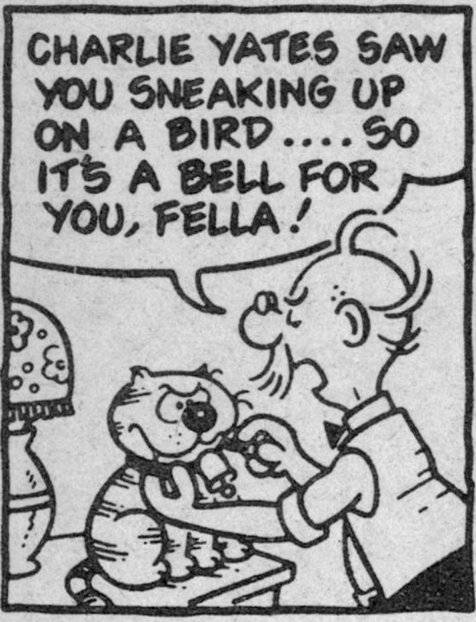
CHARLIE YATES SAW YOU SNEAKING UP ON A BIRD.... SO IT'S A BELL FOR YOU, FELLA!

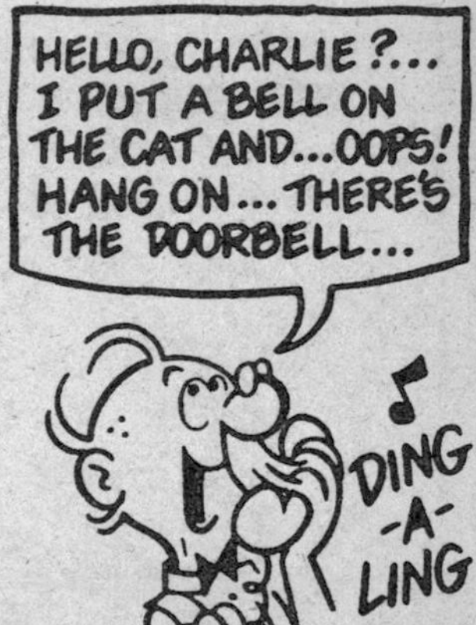
HELLO, CHARLIE?... I PUT A BELL ON THE CAT AND...OOPS! HANG ON... THERE'S THE DOORBELL...
DING -A- LING

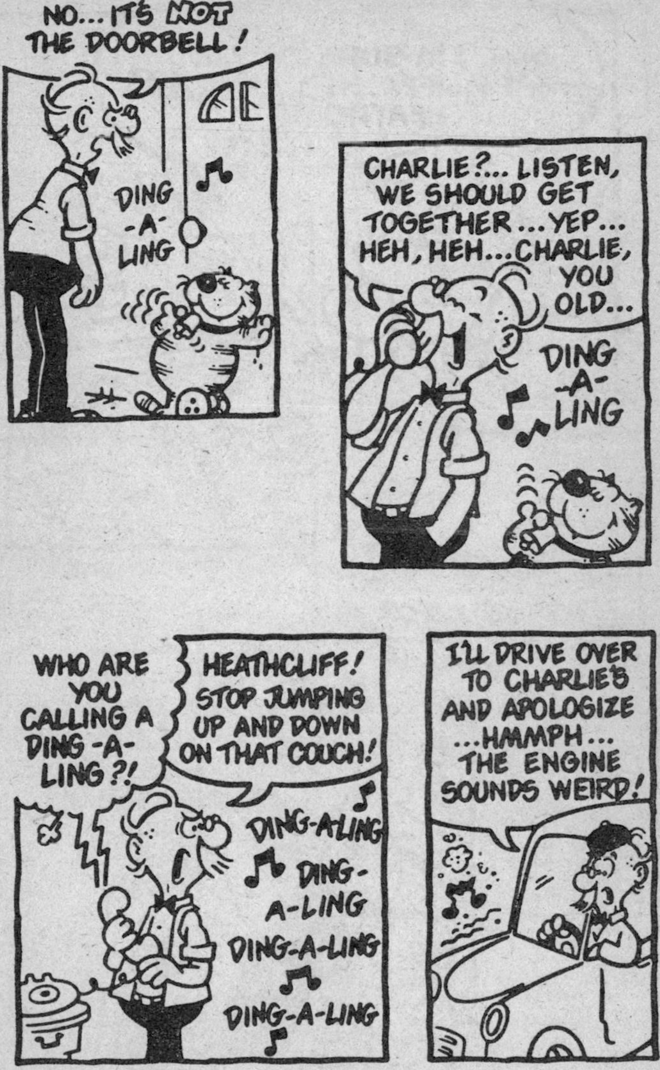
NO... IT'S NOT THE DOORBELL!
DING -A- LING
CHARLIE?... LISTEN, WE SHOULD GET TOGETHER ... YEP... HEH, HEH... CHARLIE, YOU OLD...
DING -A- LING
WHO ARE YOU CALLING A DING -A- LING?!
HEATHCLIFF! STOP JUMPING UP AND DOWN ON THAT COUCH!
DING-A-LING
DING-A-LING
DING-A-LING
DING-A-LING
I'LL DRIVE OVER TO CHARLIE'S AND APOLOGIZE ...HMMPH... THE ENGINE SOUNDS WEIRD!

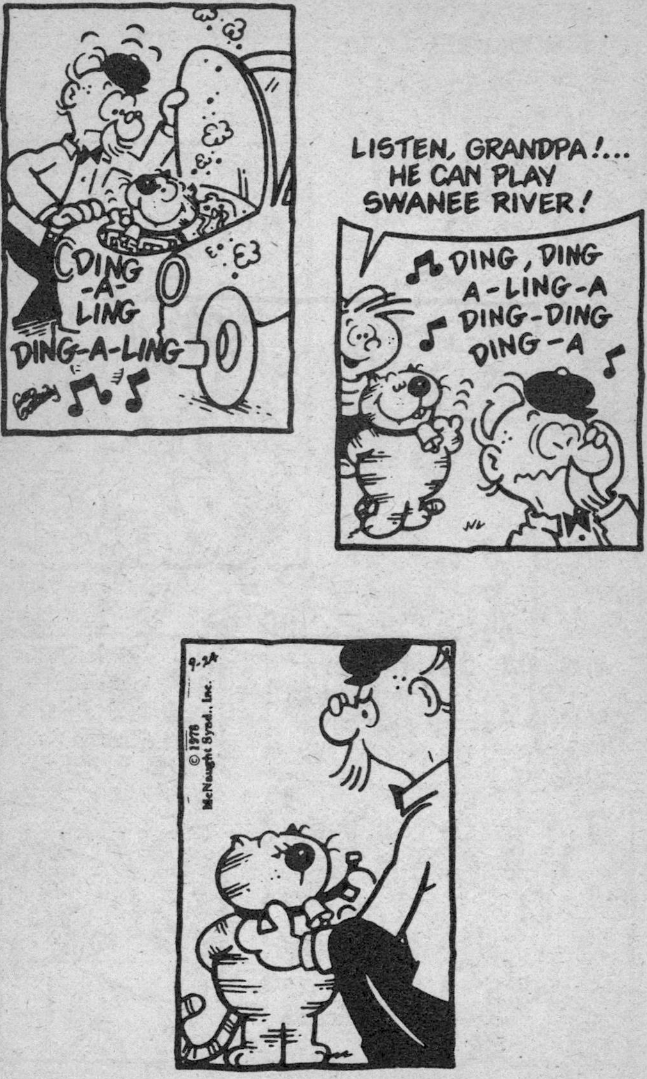
DING
-A-
LING
DING-A-LING
LISTEN, GRANDPA!... HE CAN PLAY SWANEE RIVER!
DING, DING A-LING-A DING-DING DING-A
9-24
© 1978 McNaught Synd., Inc.

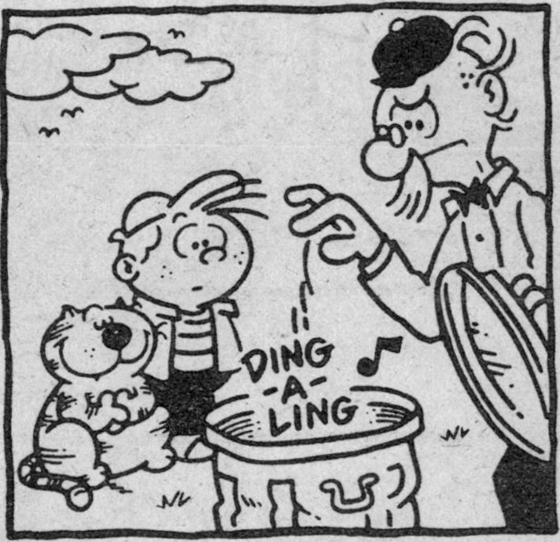
DING
-A-
LING

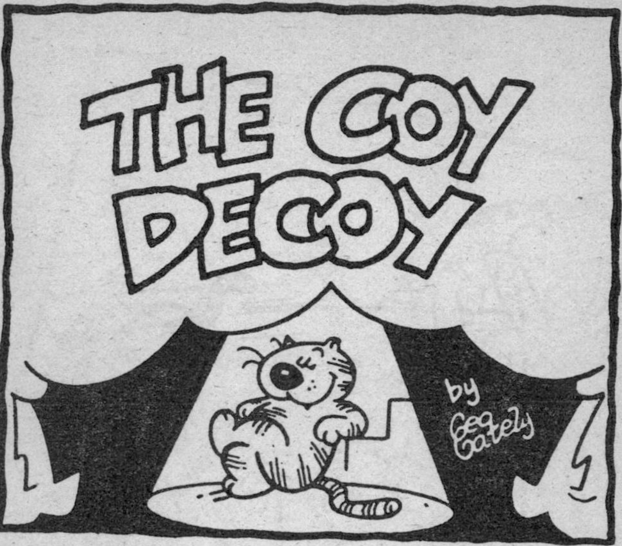
THE COY DECOY
by Geo Gately

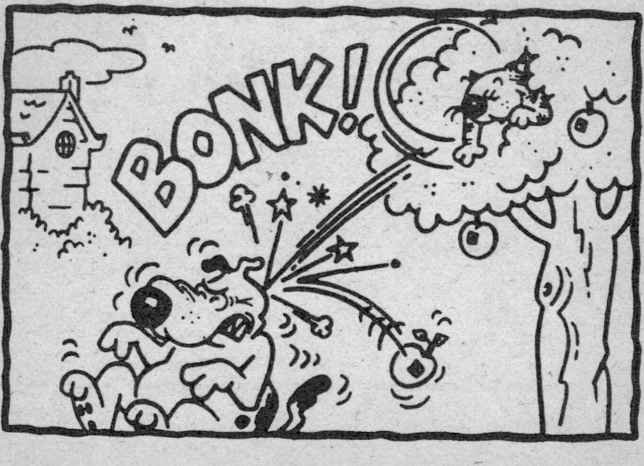
BONK!

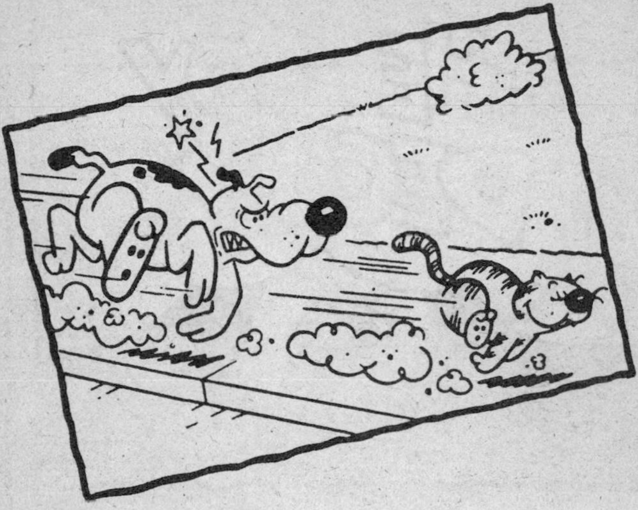

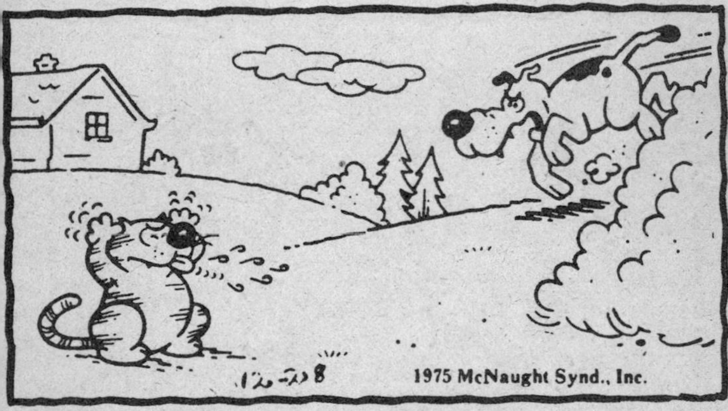
1975 McNaught Synd., Inc.

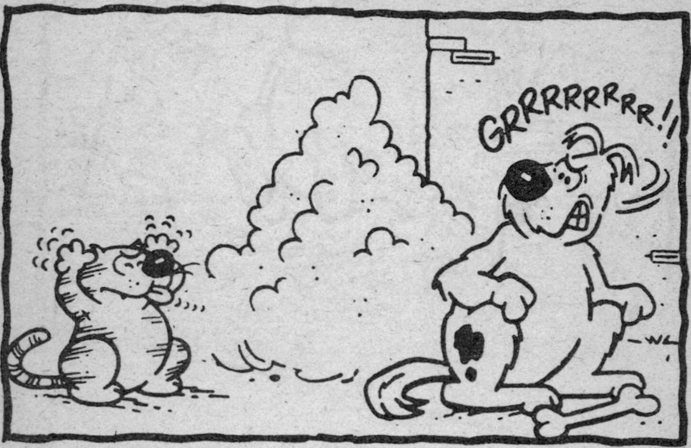
GRRRRRRRR!!

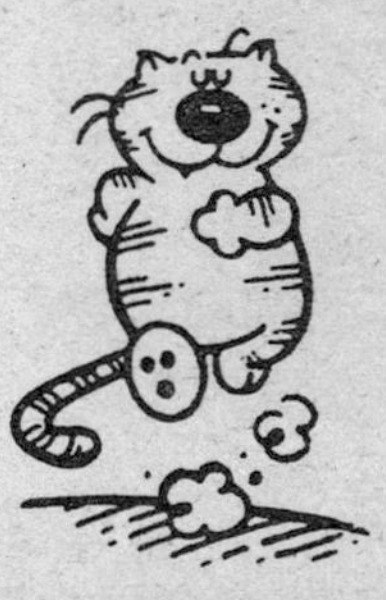

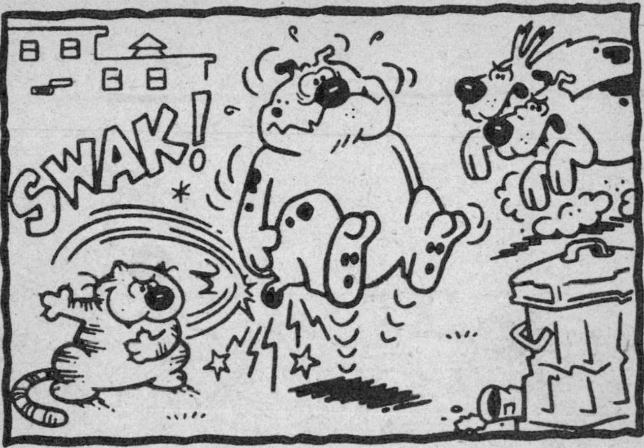
SWAK!

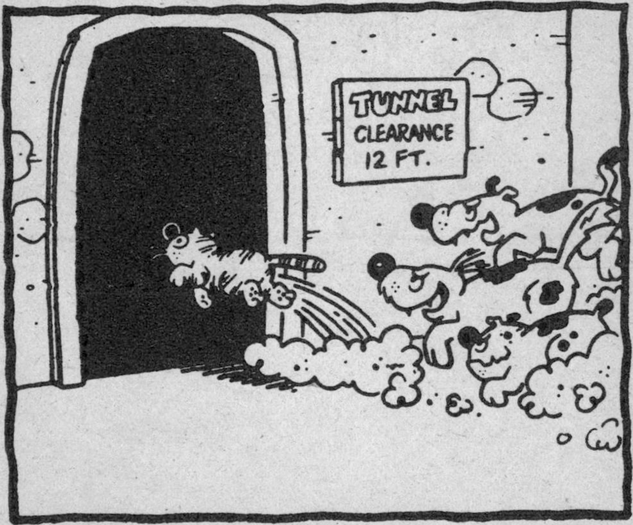
TUNNEL
CLEARANCE
12 FT.

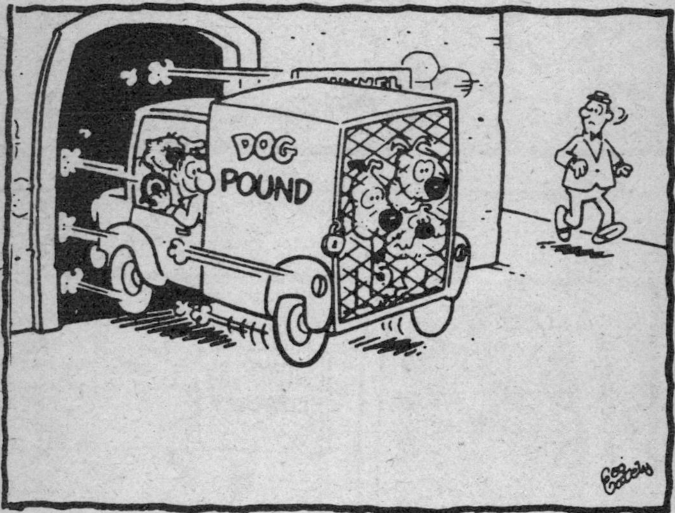
DOG
POUND

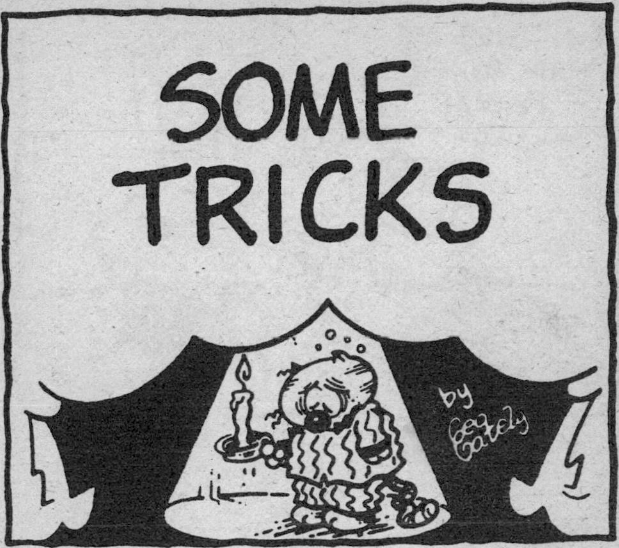
SOME
TRICKS
by

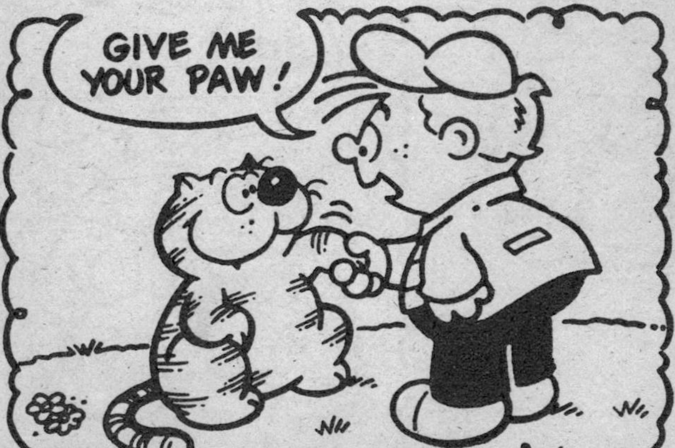
GIVE ME YOUR PAW!

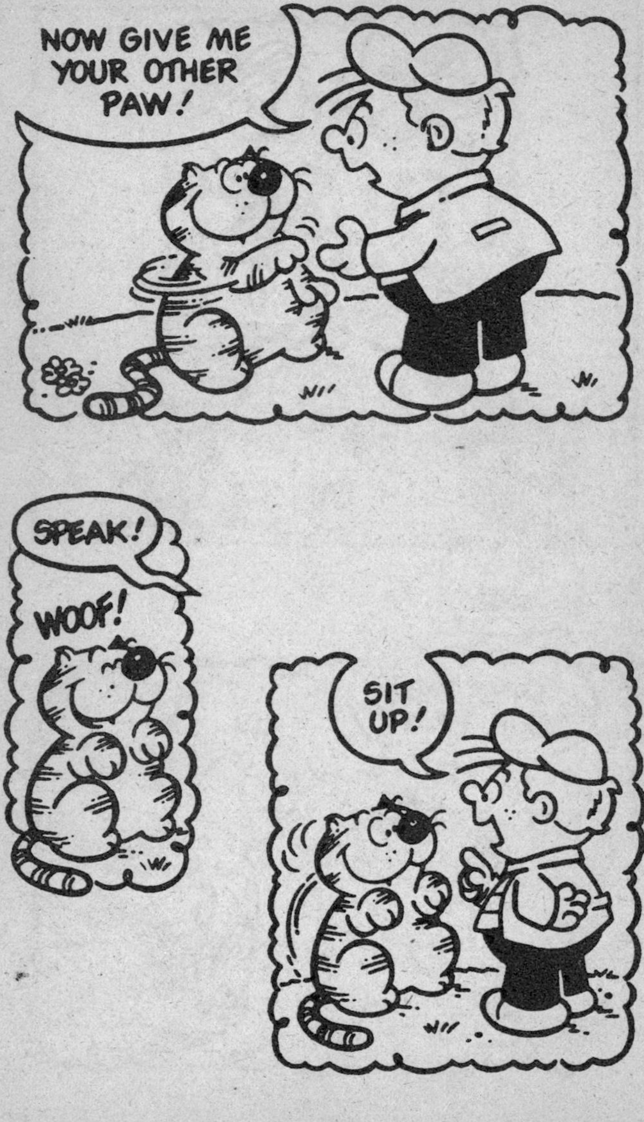
NOW GIVE ME YOUR OTHER PAW!
SPEAK!
WOOF!
SIT UP!

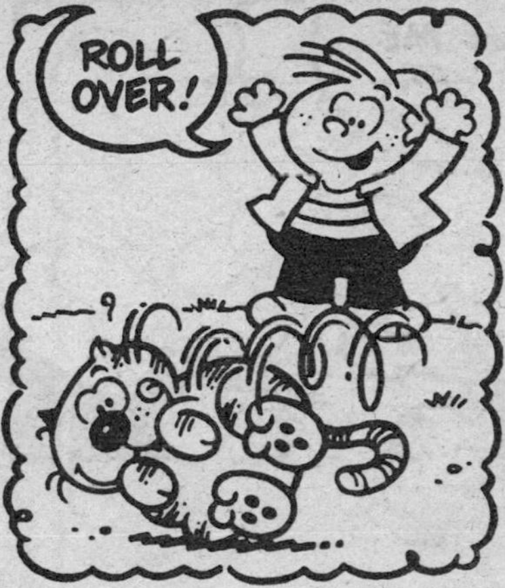
ROLL OVER!

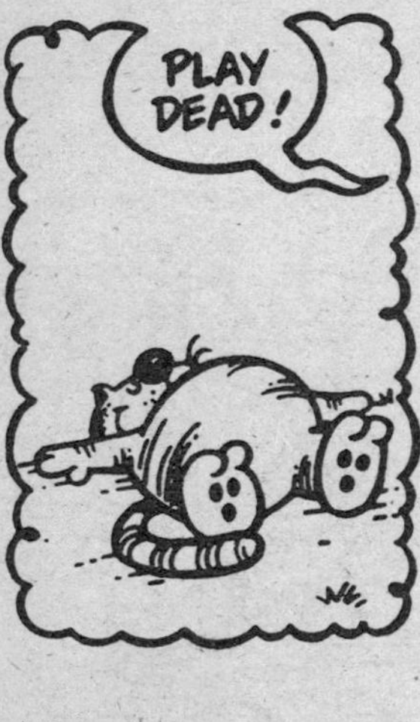
PLAY DEAD!

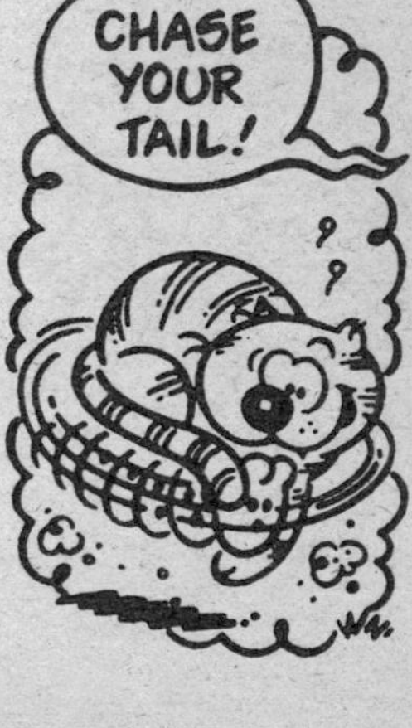
CHASE YOUR TAIL!

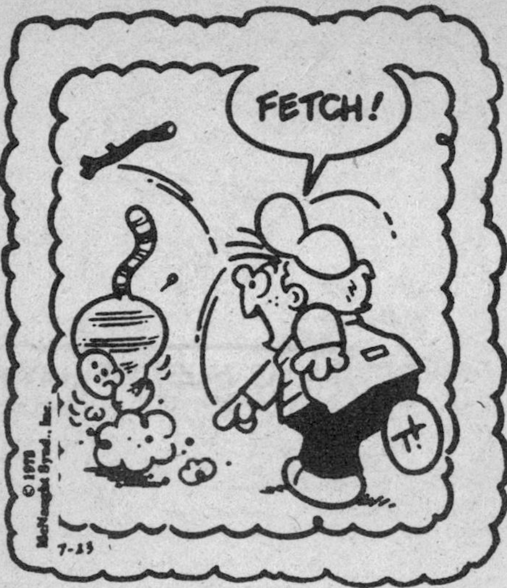
FETCH!
© 1978 McNaught Synd., Inc.
7-23

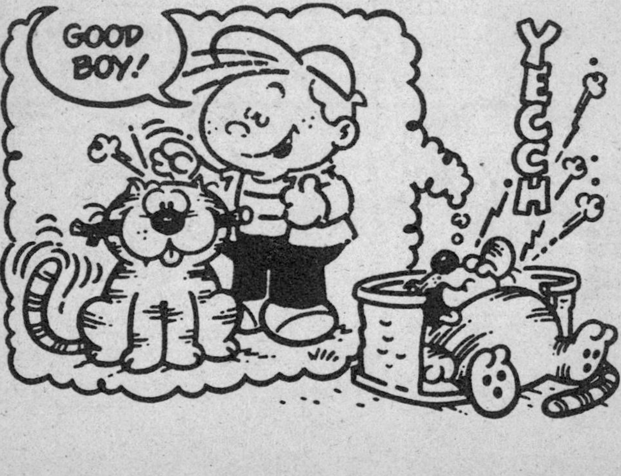
GOOD BOY!
YECCH

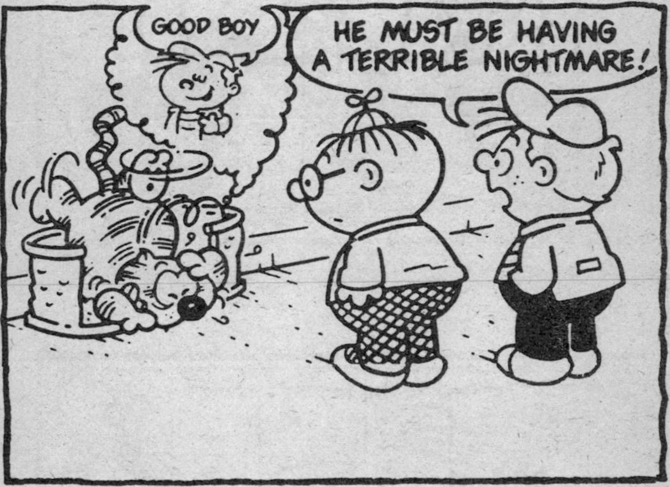
GOOD BOY
HE MUST BE HAVING A TERRIBLE NIGHTMARE!

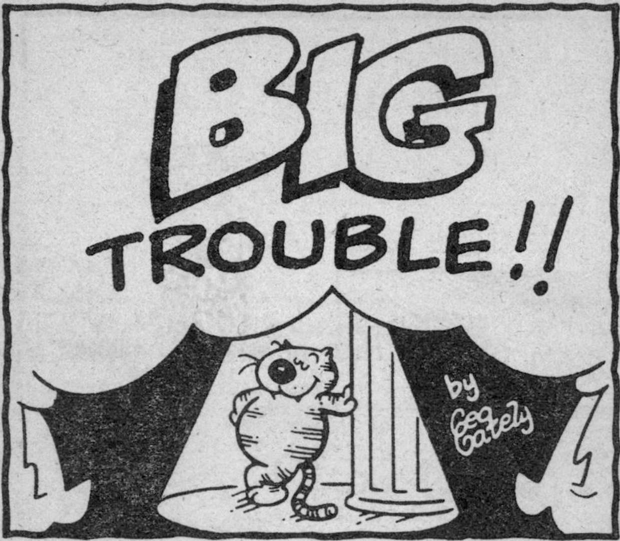
BIG
TROUBLE!!
by
Geo Gately

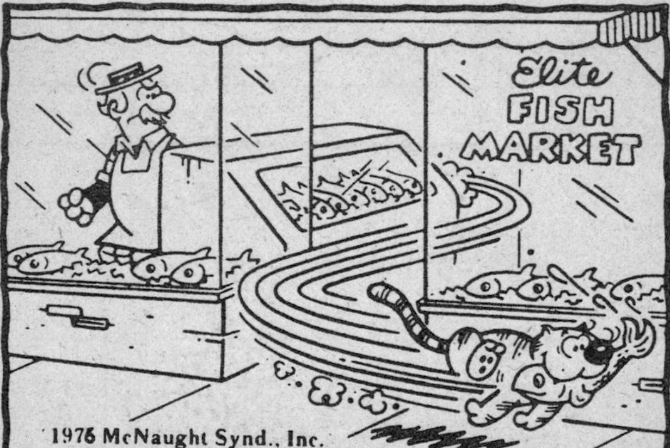
Elite
FISH
MARKET
1976 McNaught Synd., Inc.

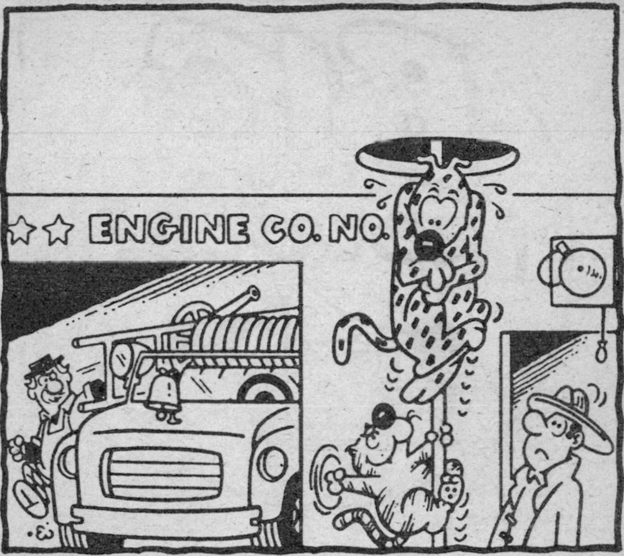
ENGINE CO. NO.

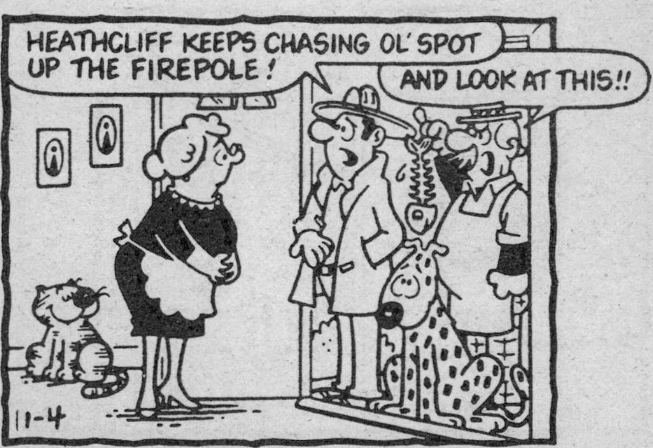
HEATHCLIFF KEEPS CHASING OL' SPOT UP THE FIREPOLE!
AND LOOK AT THIS!!
11-4

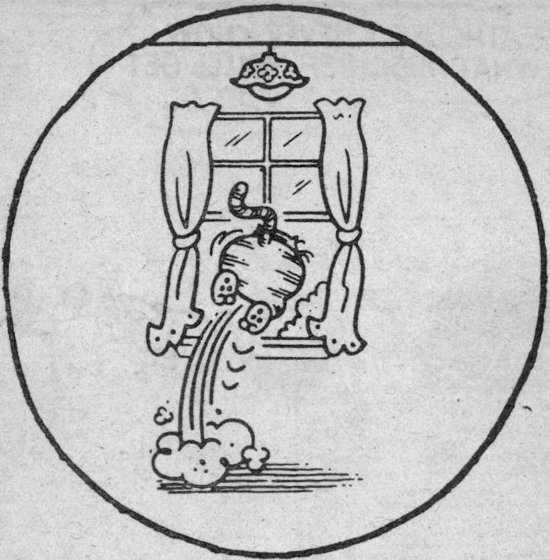

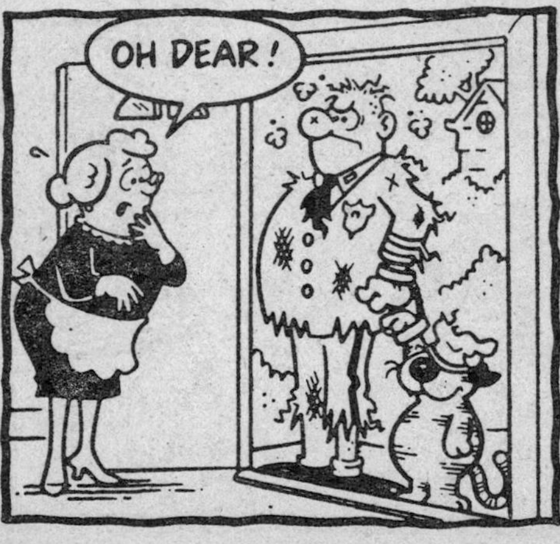
OH DEAR!

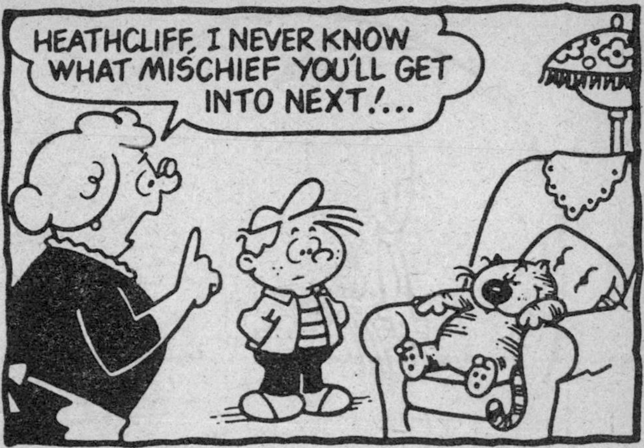
HEATHCLIFF, I NEVER KNOW WHAT MISCHIEF YOU'LL GET INTO NEXT!...

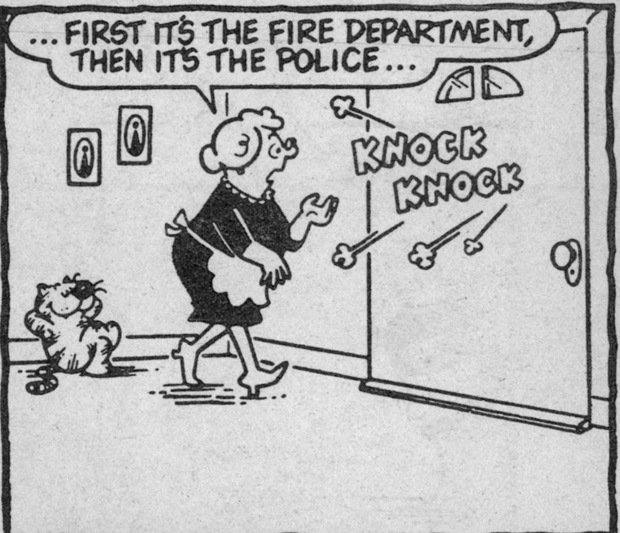
...FIRST IT'S THE FIRE DEPARTMENT, THEN IT'S THE POLICE...
KNOCK
KNOCK

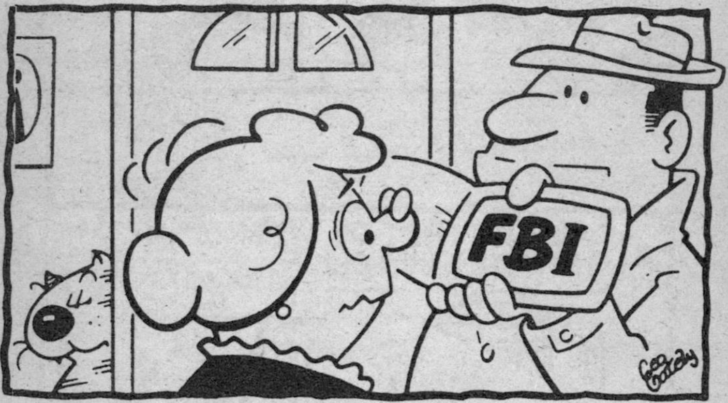
FBI

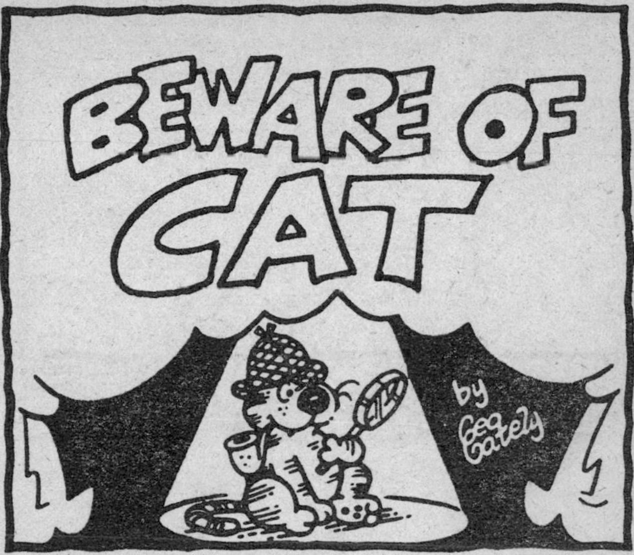
BEWARE OF CAT
by Geo Gately

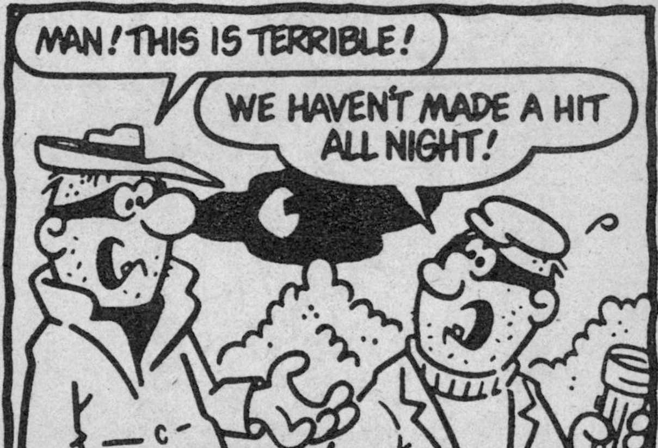
MAN! THIS IS TERRIBLE!
WE HAVEN'T MADE A HIT ALL NIGHT!

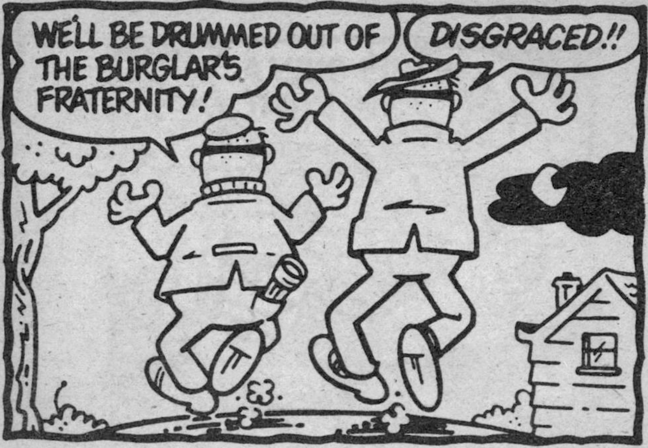
WE'LL BE DRUMMED OUT OF THE BURGLAR'S FRATERNITY!
DISGRACED!!

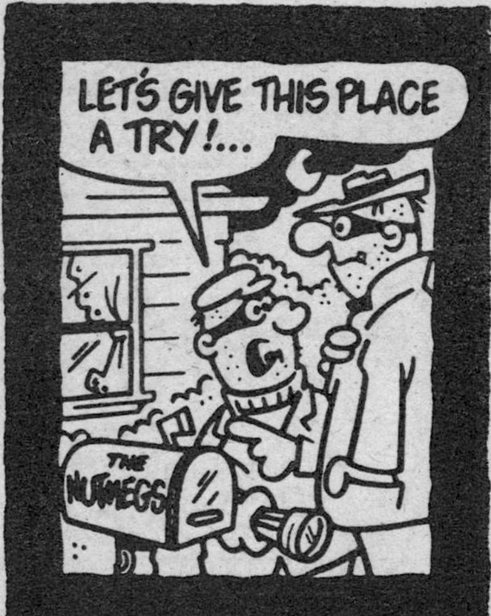
LET'S GIVE THIS PLACE A TRY!...
THE NUTMEGS

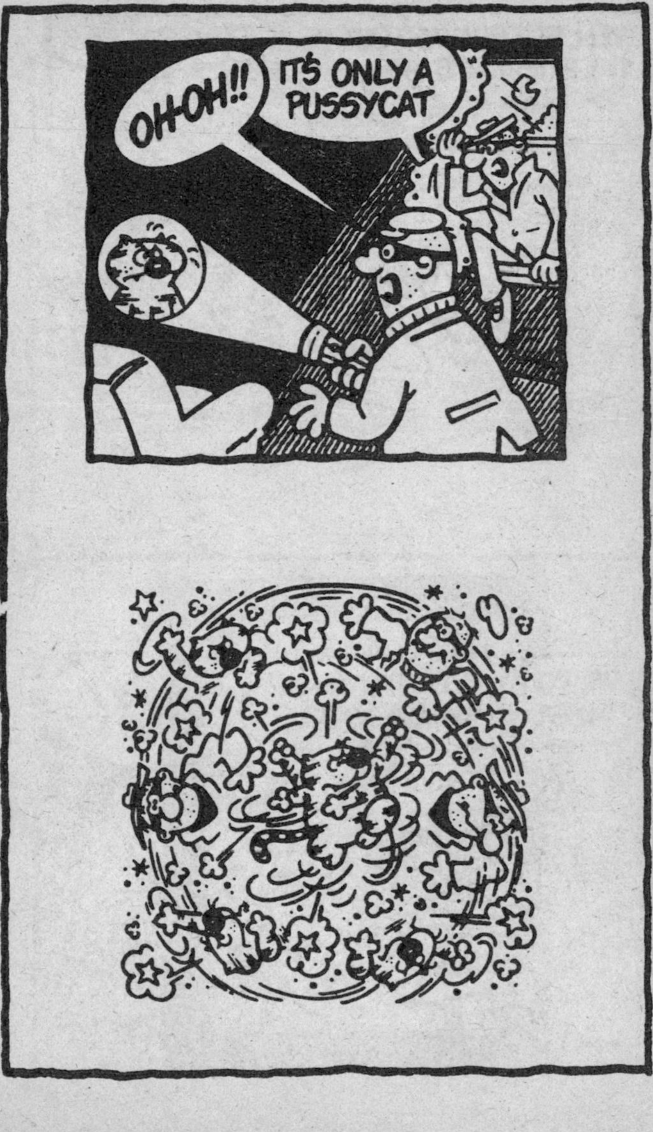
OH-OH!!
IT'S ONLY A PUSSYCAT

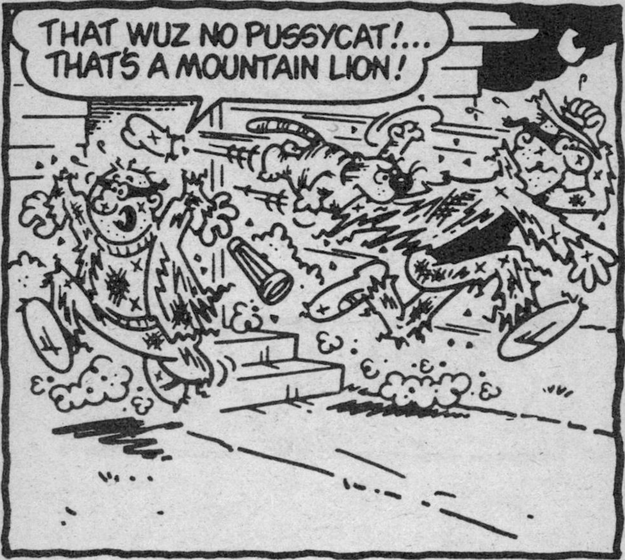
THAT WUZ NO PUSSYCAT!... THAT'S A MOUNTAIN LION!

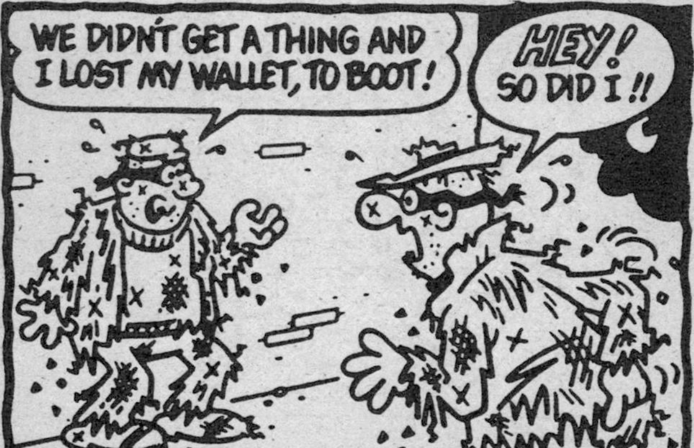
WE DIDN'T GET A THING AND I LOST MY WALLET, TO BOOT!
HEY! SO DID I!!

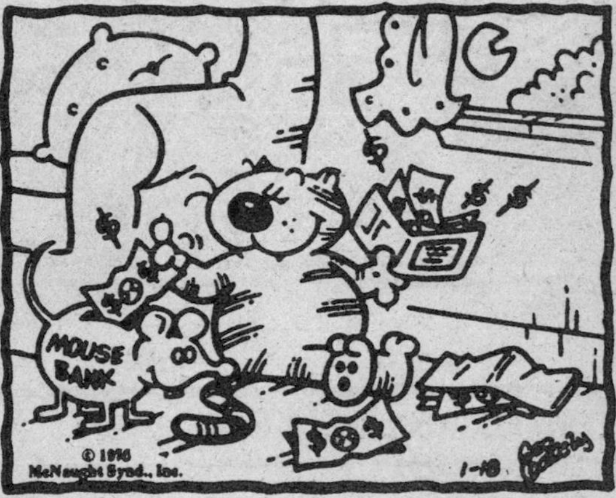
MOUSE BANK
© 1976 McNaught Synd., Inc.
1-18

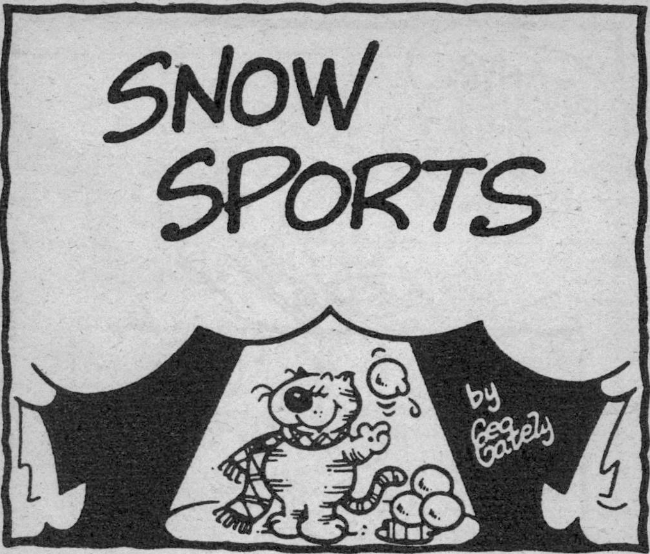
SNOW SPORTS
by Geo Gately

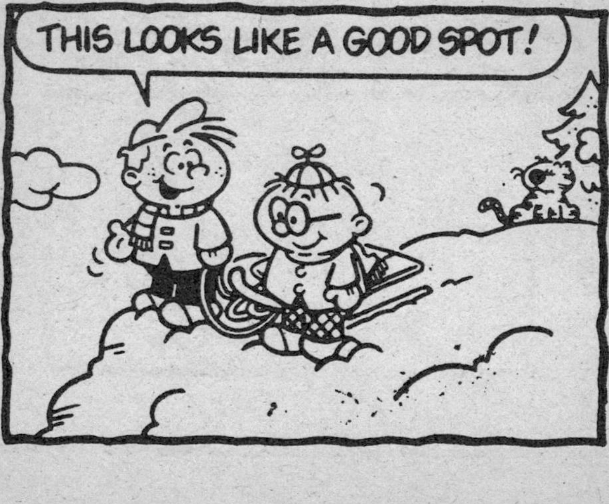
THIS LOOKS LIKE A GOOD SPOT!

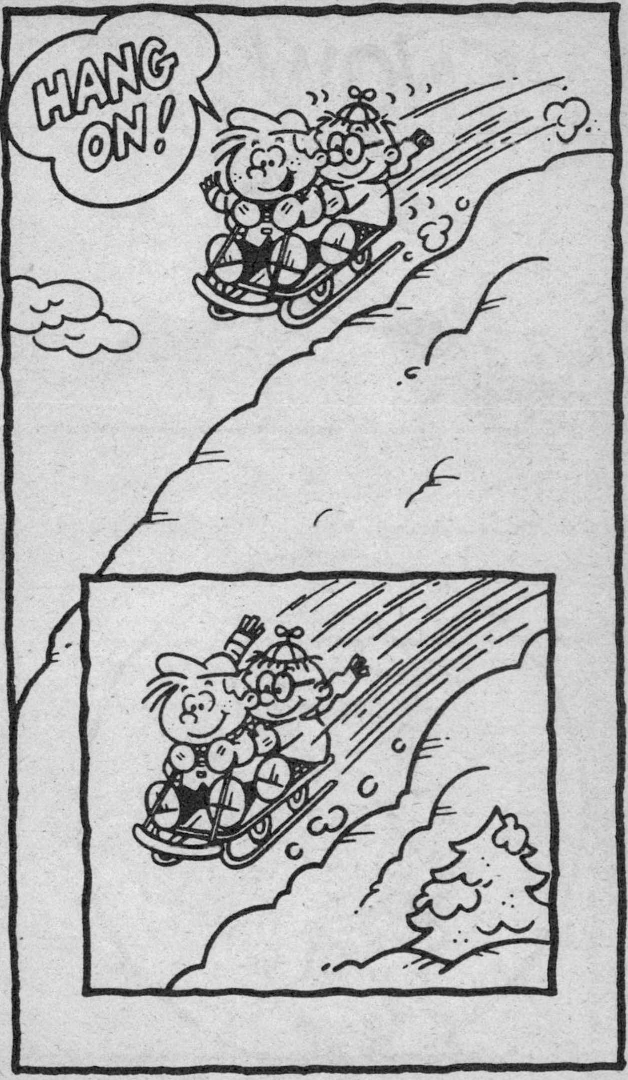
HANG ON!

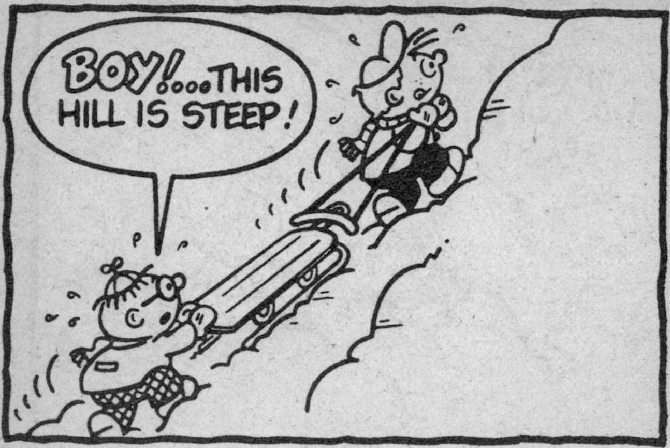
BOY!....THIS HILL IS STEEP!

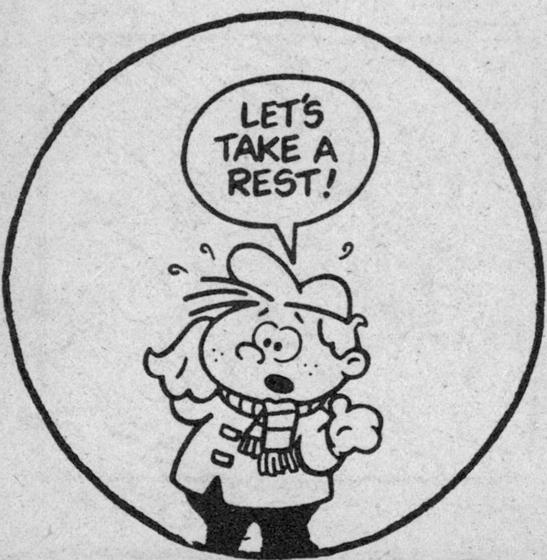
LET'S TAKE A REST!

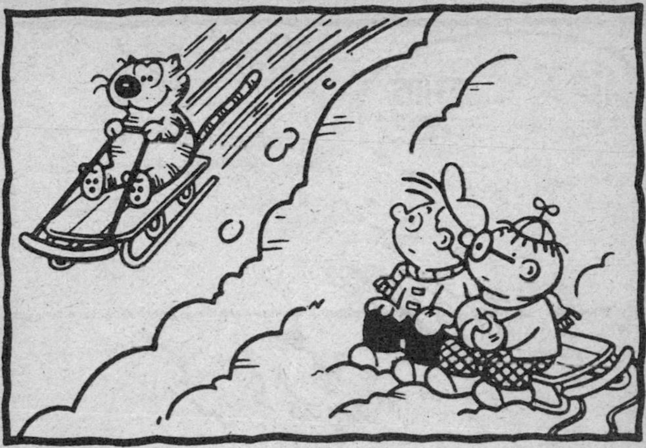

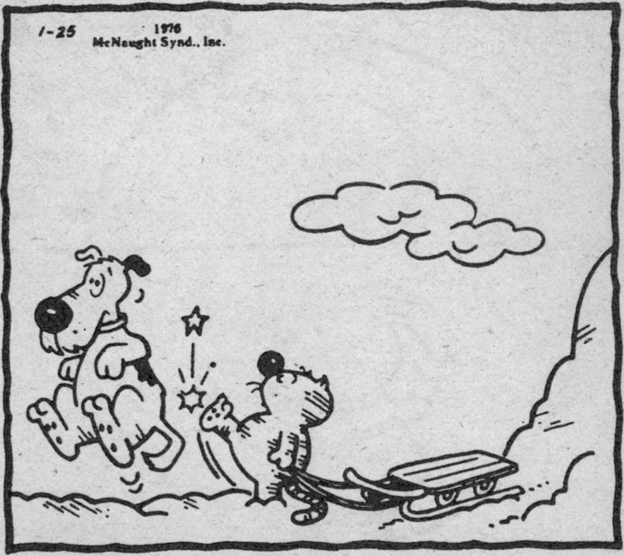
1-25
1976
McNaught Synd., Inc.

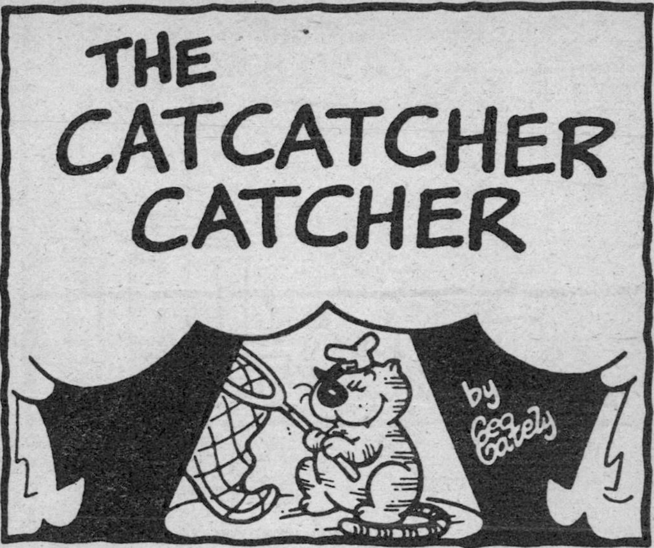
THE CATCATCHER CATCHER
by Geo Gately

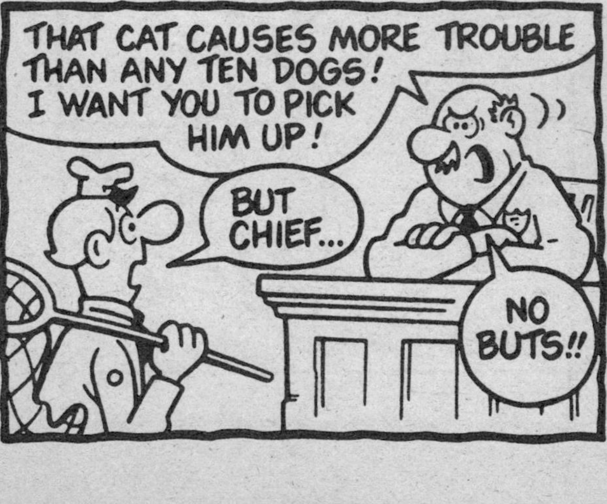
THAT CAT CAUSES MORE TROUBLE THAN ANY TEN DOGS! I WANT YOU TO PICK HIM UP!
BUT CHIEF...
NO BUTS!!

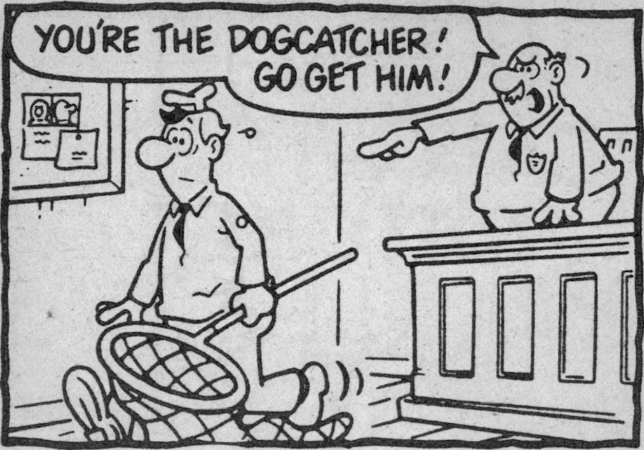
YOU'RE THE DOGCATCHER! GO GET HIM!

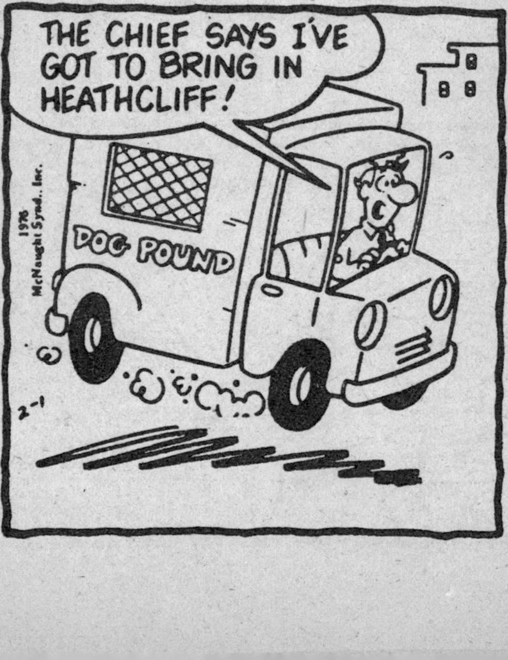
THE CHIEF SAYS I'VE GOT TO BRING IN HEATHCLIFF!
DOG POUND
2-1

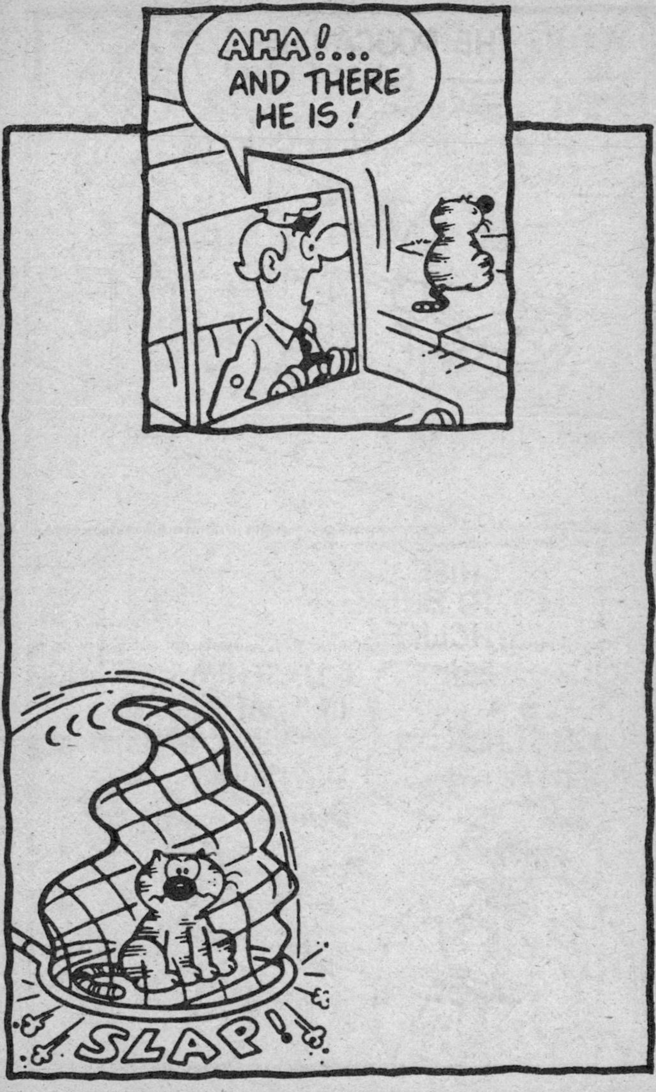
AHA!... AND THERE HE IS!
SLAP!

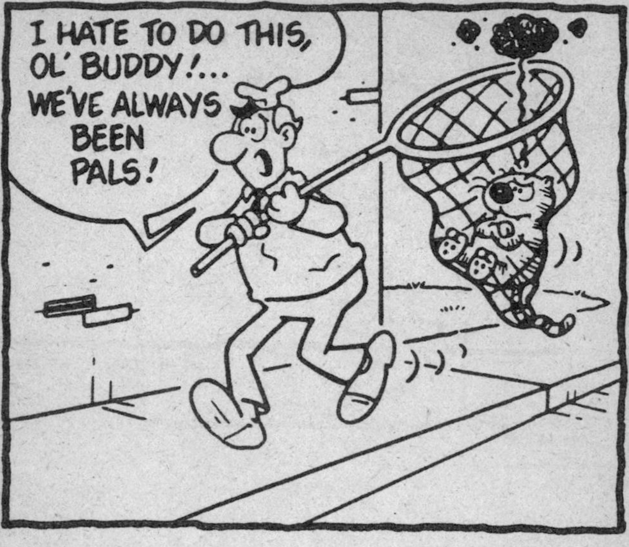
I HATE TO DO THIS, OL' BUDDY!... WE'VE ALWAYS BEEN PALS!

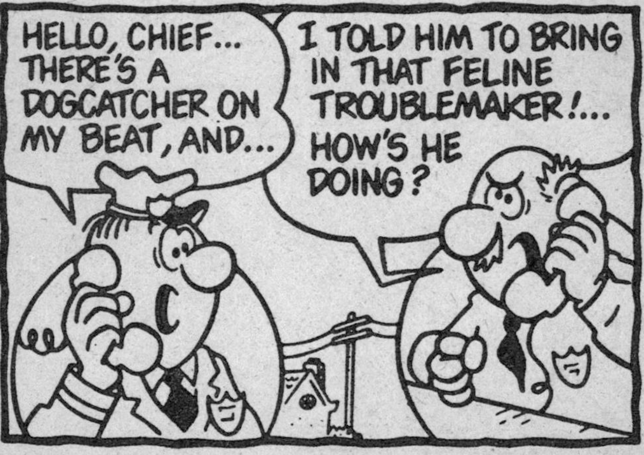
HELLO, CHIEF... THERE'S A DOGCATCHER ON MY BEAT, AND...
I TOLD HIM TO BRING IN THAT FELINE TROUBLEMAKER!... HOW'S HE DOING?

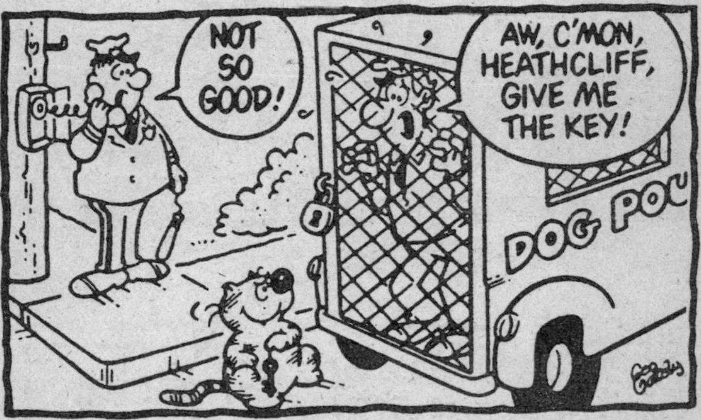
NOT SO GOOD!
AW, C'MON, HEATHCLIFF, GIVE ME THE KEY!
DOG POU

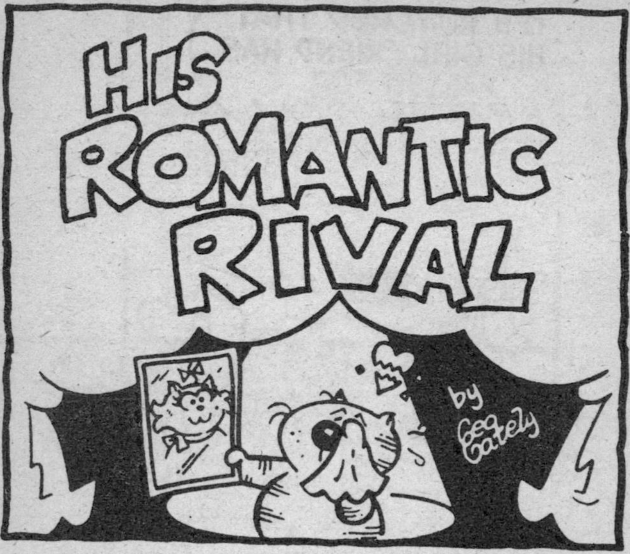
HIS ROMANTIC RIVAL
by Geo Gately

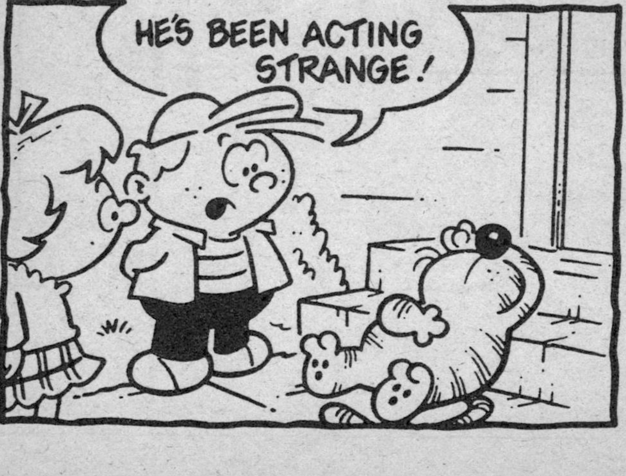
HE'S BEEN ACTING STRANGE!

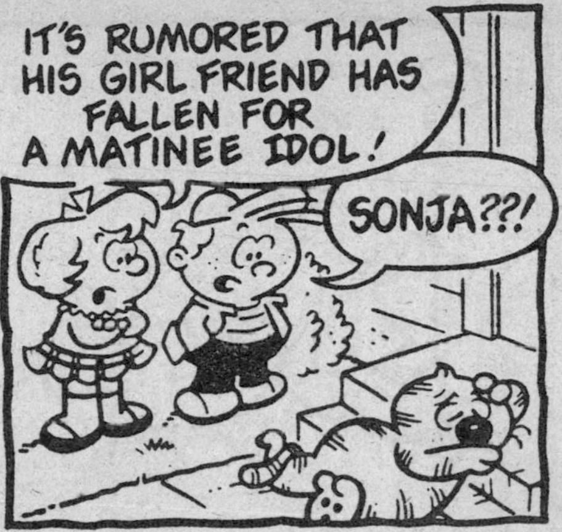
IT'S RUMORED THAT HIS GIRL FRIEND HAS FALLEN FOR A MATINEE IDOL!
SONJA??!

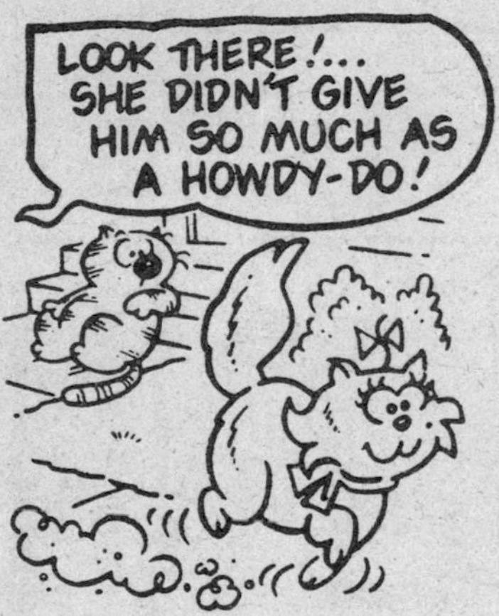
LOOK THERE!... SHE DIDN'T GIVE HIM SO MUCH AS A HOWDY-DO!

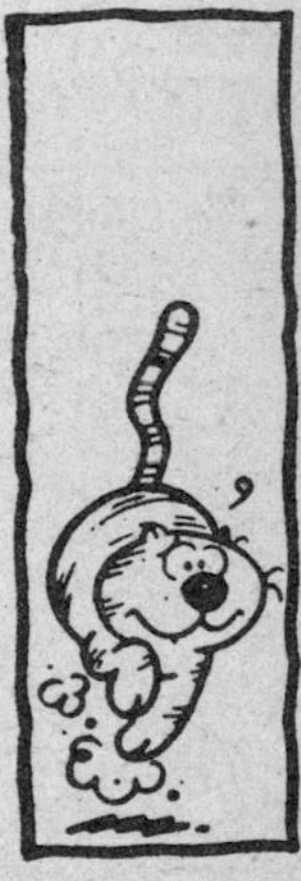

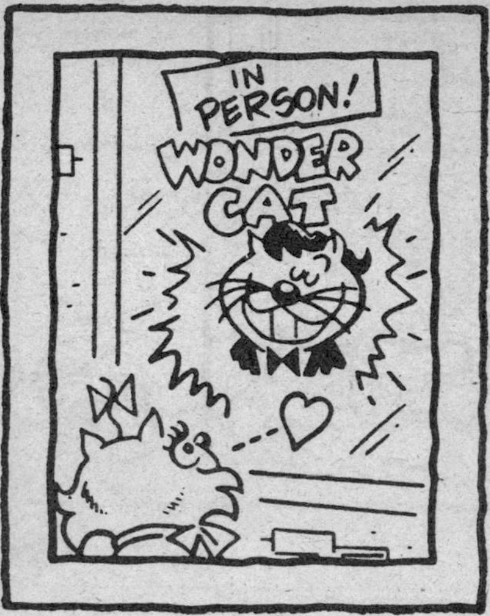
IN PERSON!
WONDER CAT

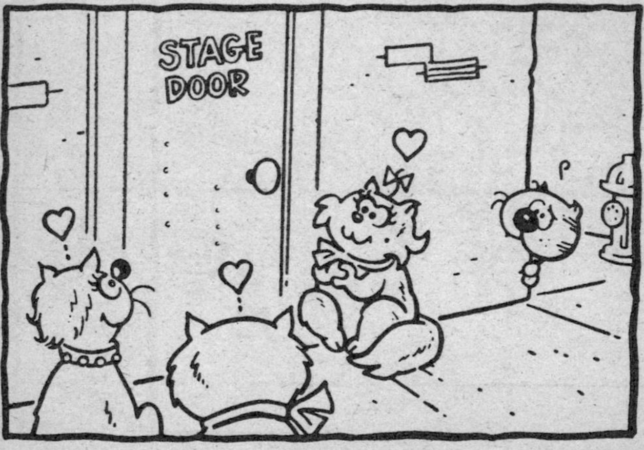
STAGE DOOR

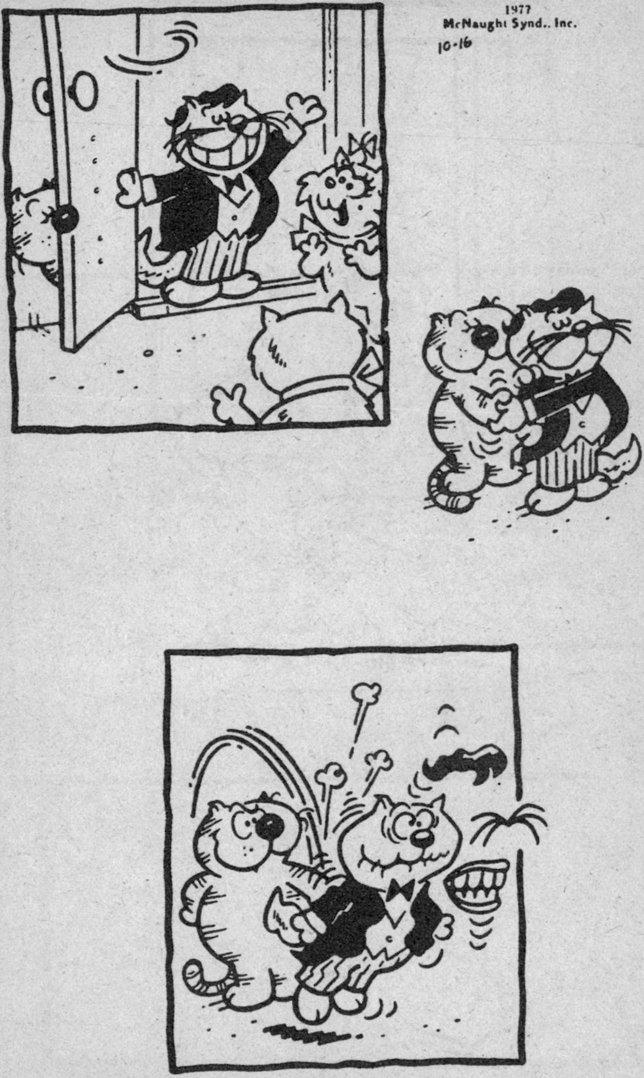
1977
McNaught Synd., Inc.
10-16

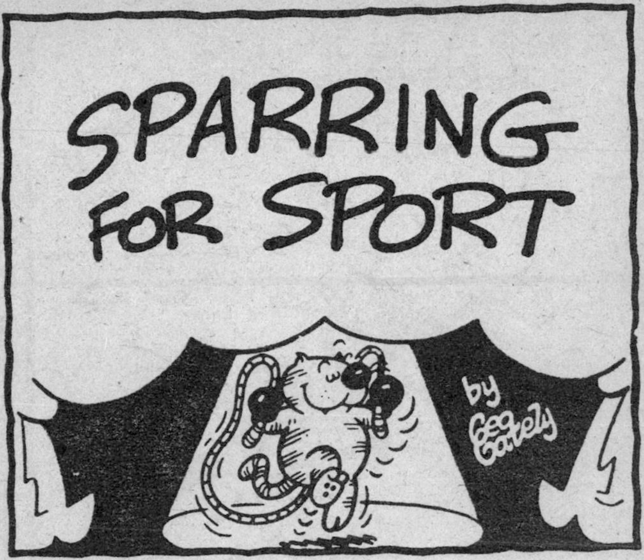
SPARRING
FOR SPORT
by Geo Gately

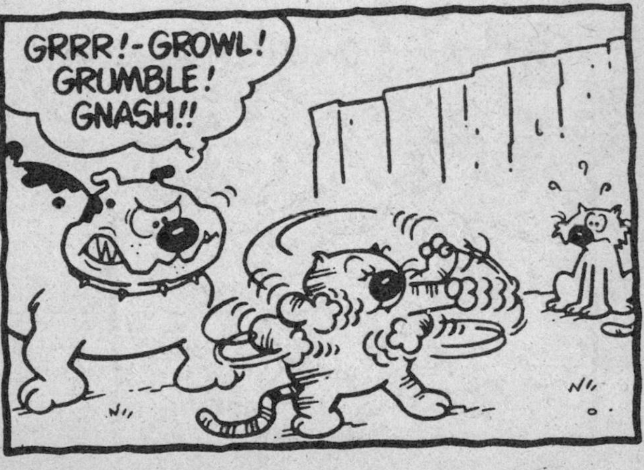
GRRR!-GROWL! GRUMBLE! GNASH!!

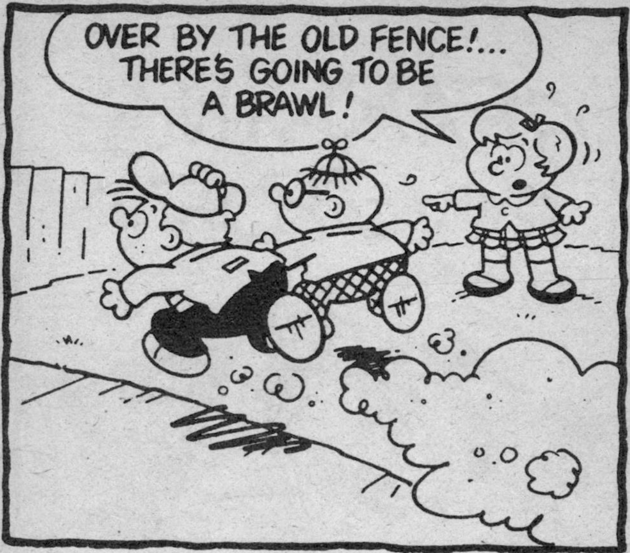
OVER BY THE OLD FENCE!... THERE'S GOING TO BE A BRAWL!

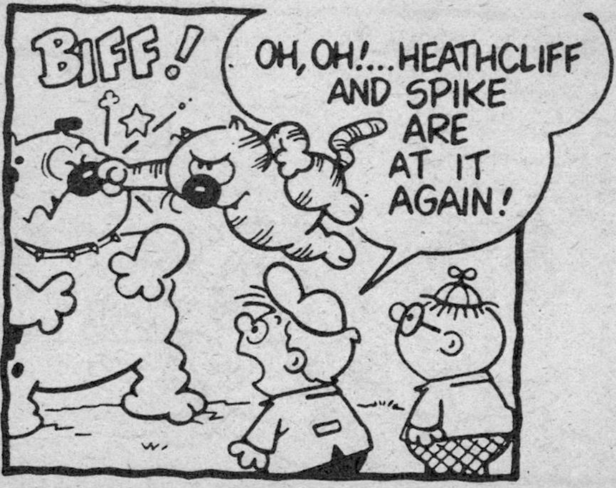
BIFF!
OH, OH!... HEATHCLIFF AND SPIKE ARE AT IT AGAIN!

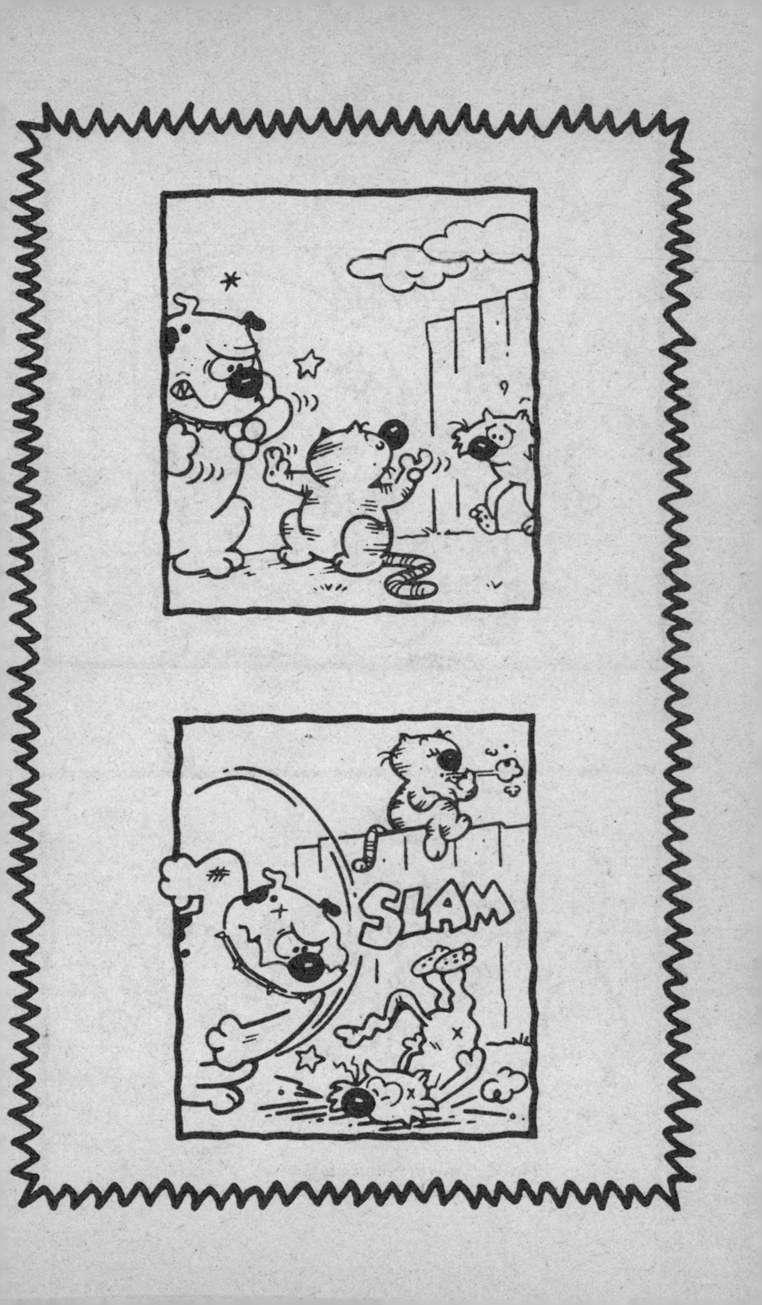
SLAM

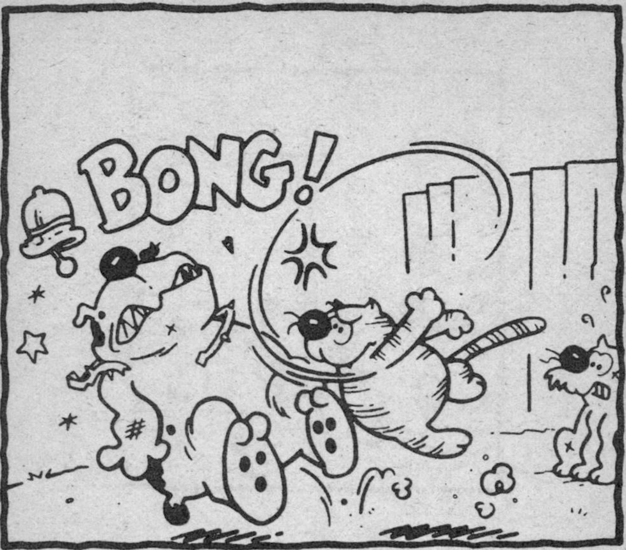
BONG!

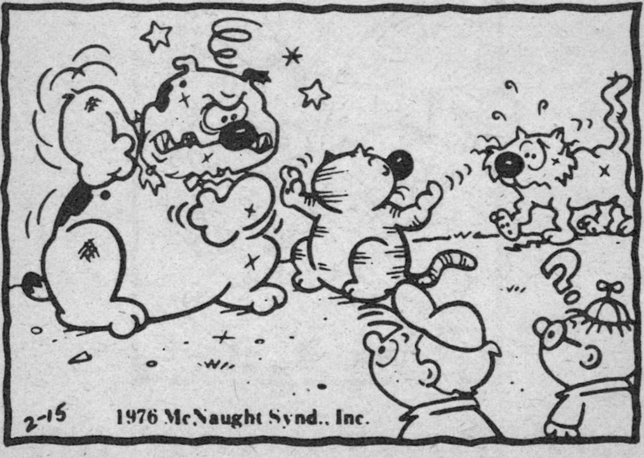
2-15
1976 McNaught Synd., Inc.

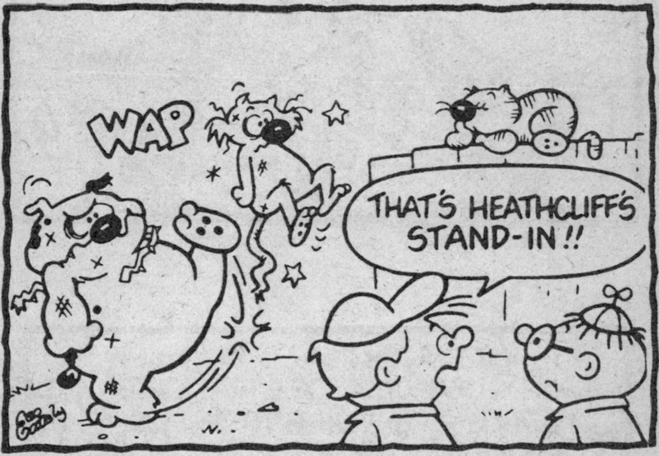
WAP
THAT'S HEATHCLIFF'S STAND-IN!!

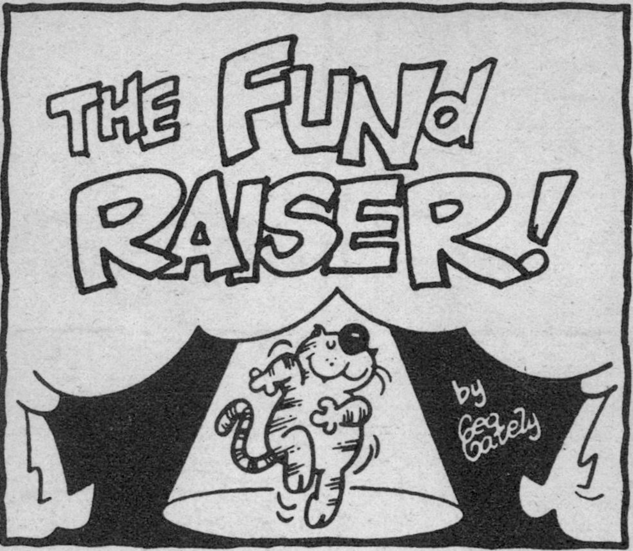
THE FUNd RAISER!
by Geo Gately

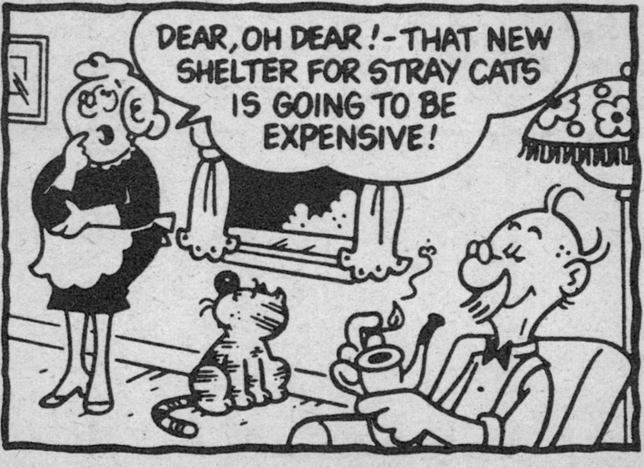
DEAR, OH DEAR! - THAT NEW SHELTER FOR STRAY CATS IS GOING TO BE EXPENSIVE!

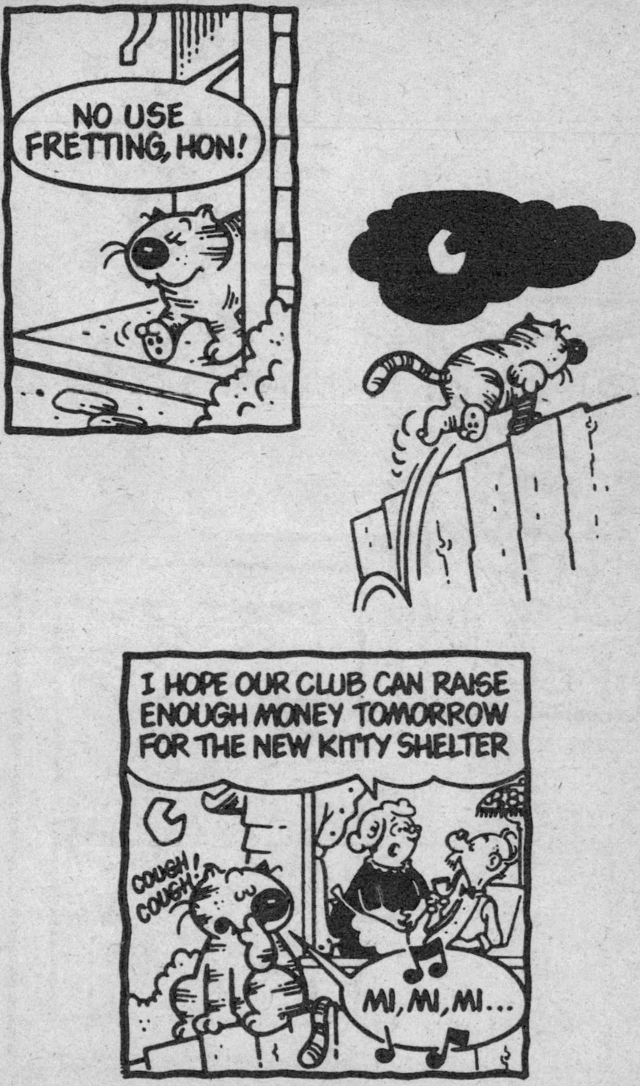
NO USE FRETTING, HON!
I HOPE OUR CLUB CAN RAISE ENOUGH MONEY TOMORROW FOR THE NEW KITTY SHELTER
COUGH! COUGH!
MI, MI, MI...

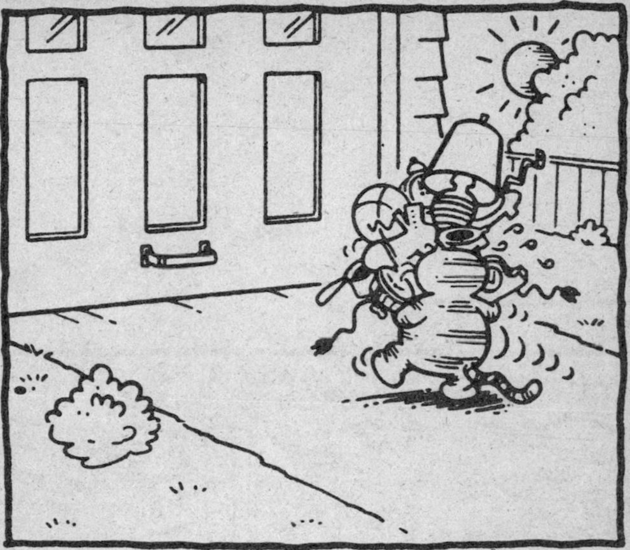

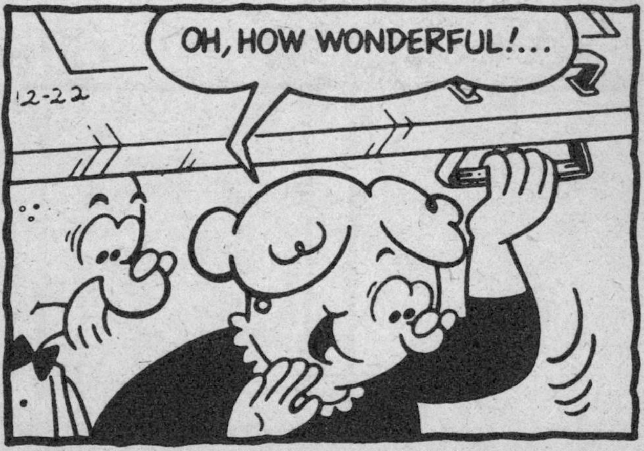
OH, HOW WONDERFUL!...
12-22

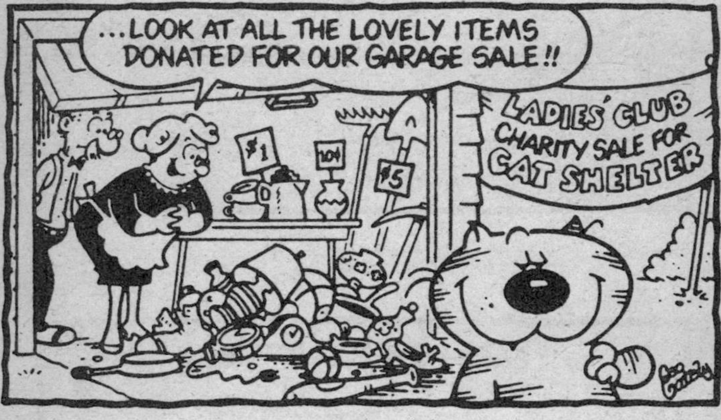
...LOOK AT ALL THE LOVELY ITEMS DONATED FOR OUR GARAGE SALE!!
LADIES' CLUB CHARITY SALE FOR CAT SHELTER
$1
10¢
$5

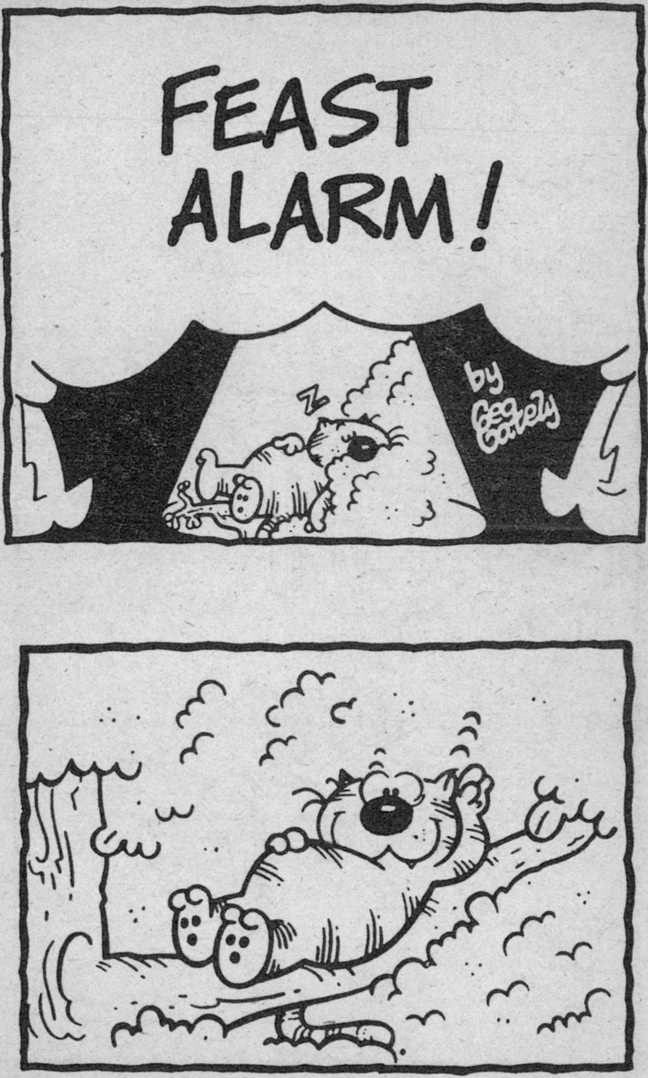
FEAST ALARM!
Z
by Geo Gately

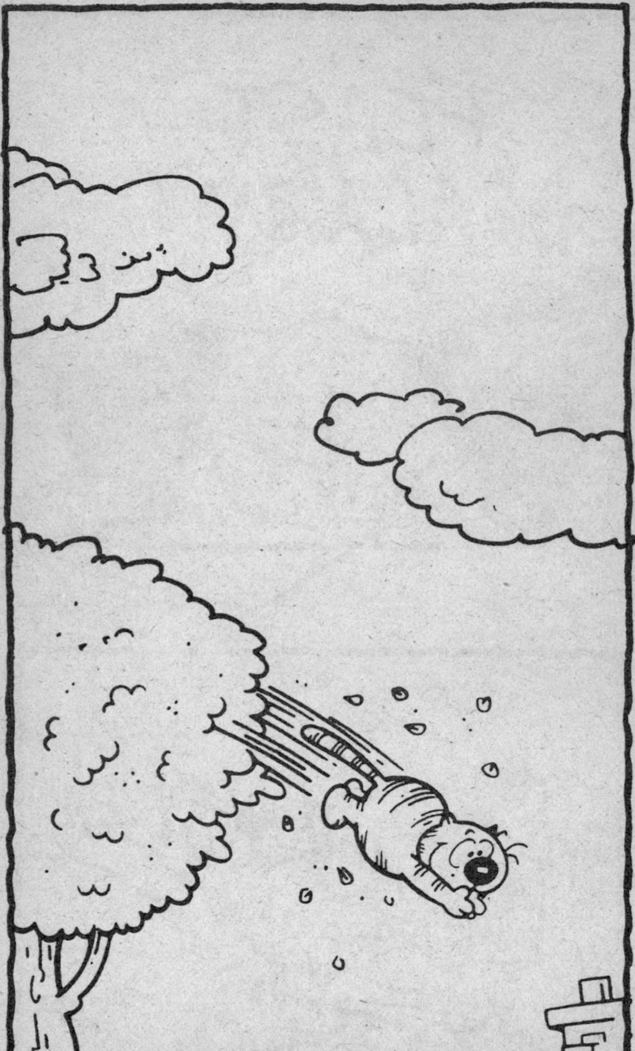

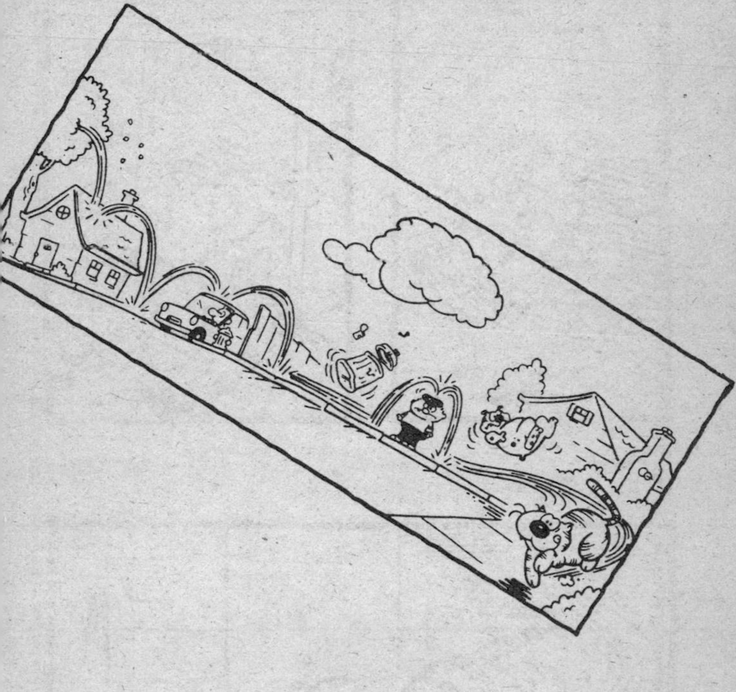

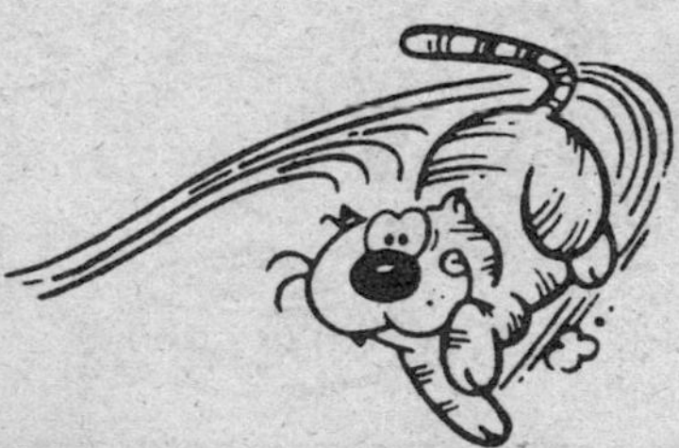

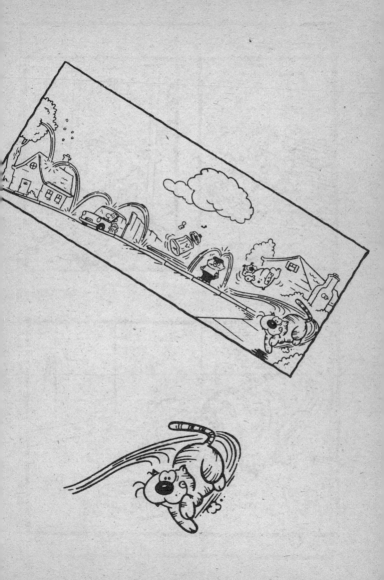

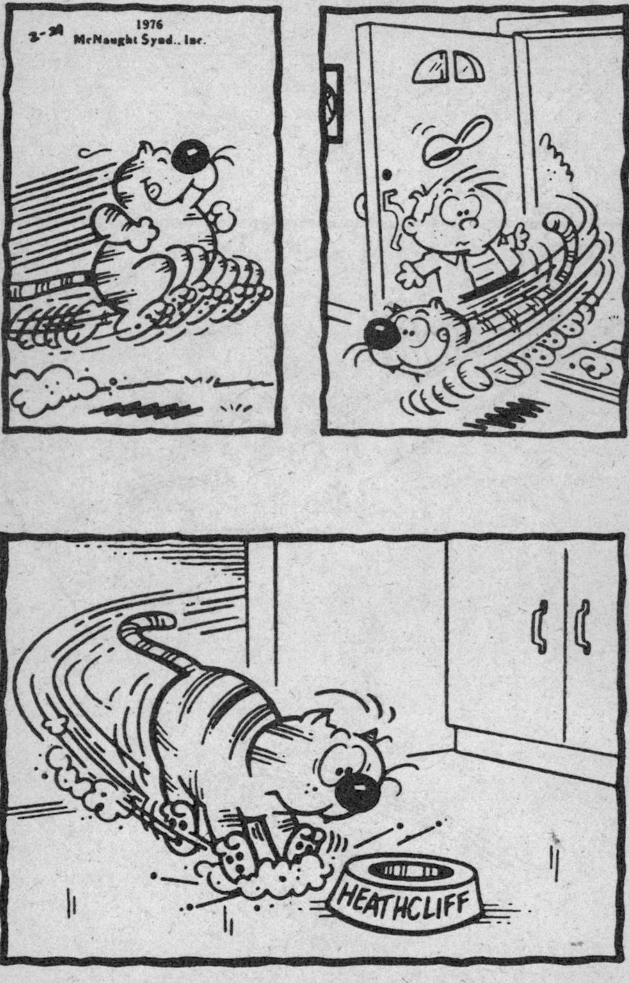
1976
McNaught Synd., Inc.
HEATHCLIFF

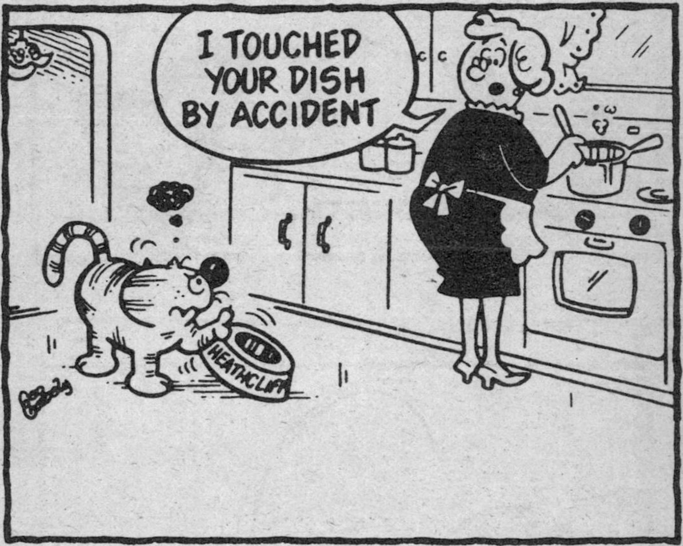
I TOUCHED YOUR DISH BY ACCIDENT
HEATHCLIFF

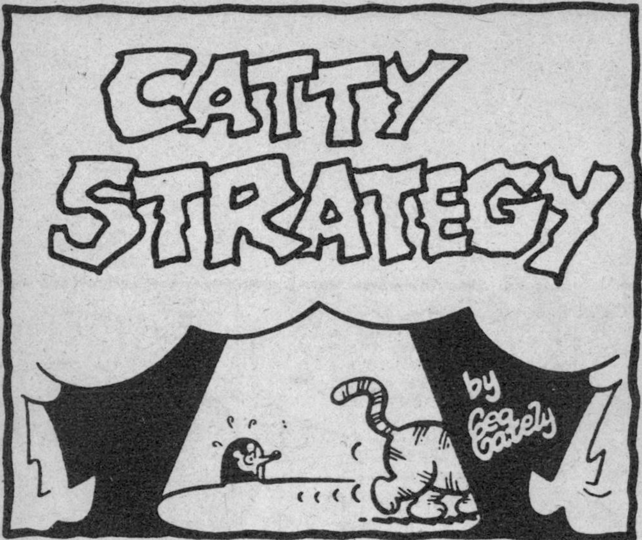
CATTY STRATEGY
by Geo Gately

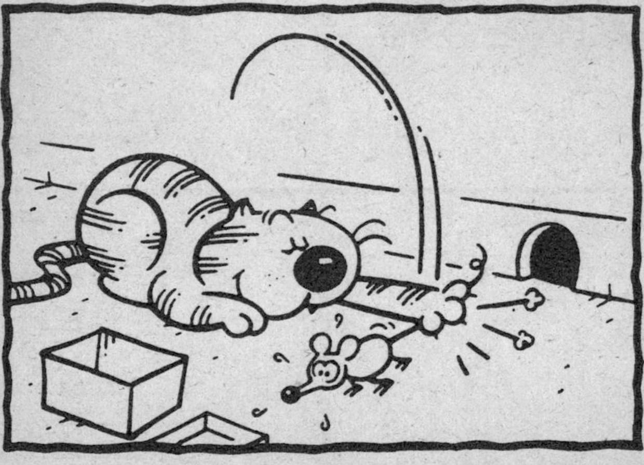

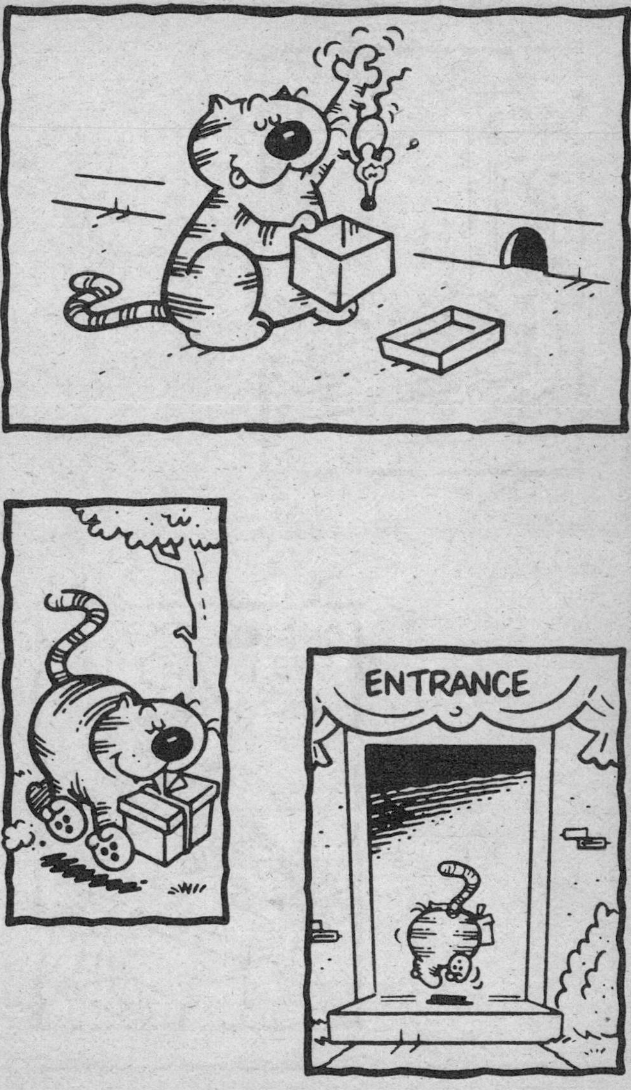
ENTRANCE

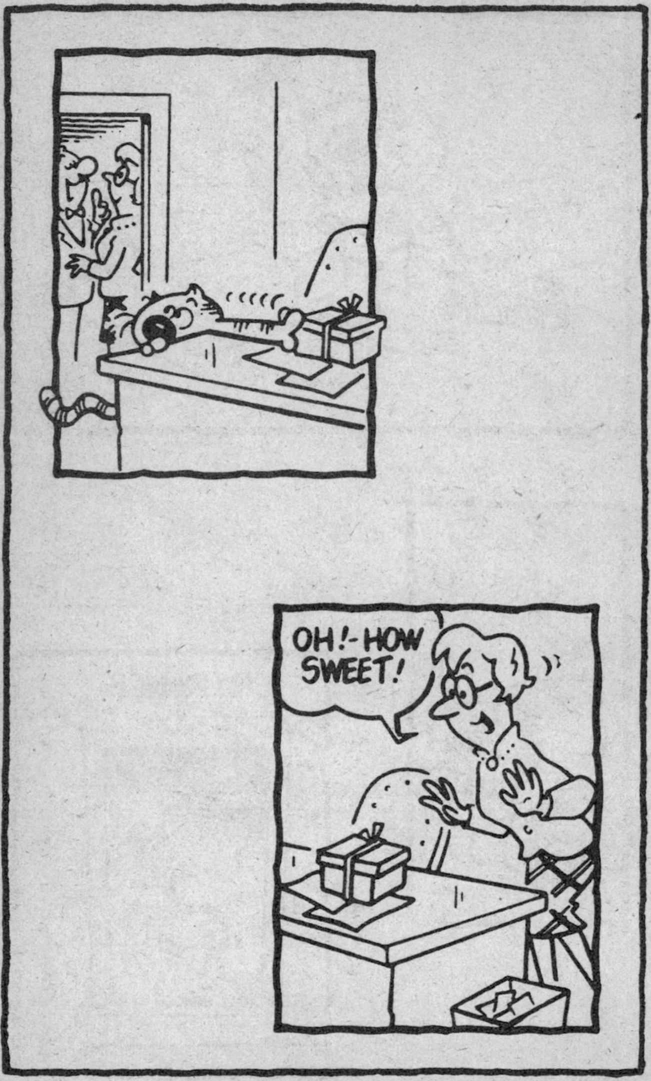
OH!-HOW SWEET!

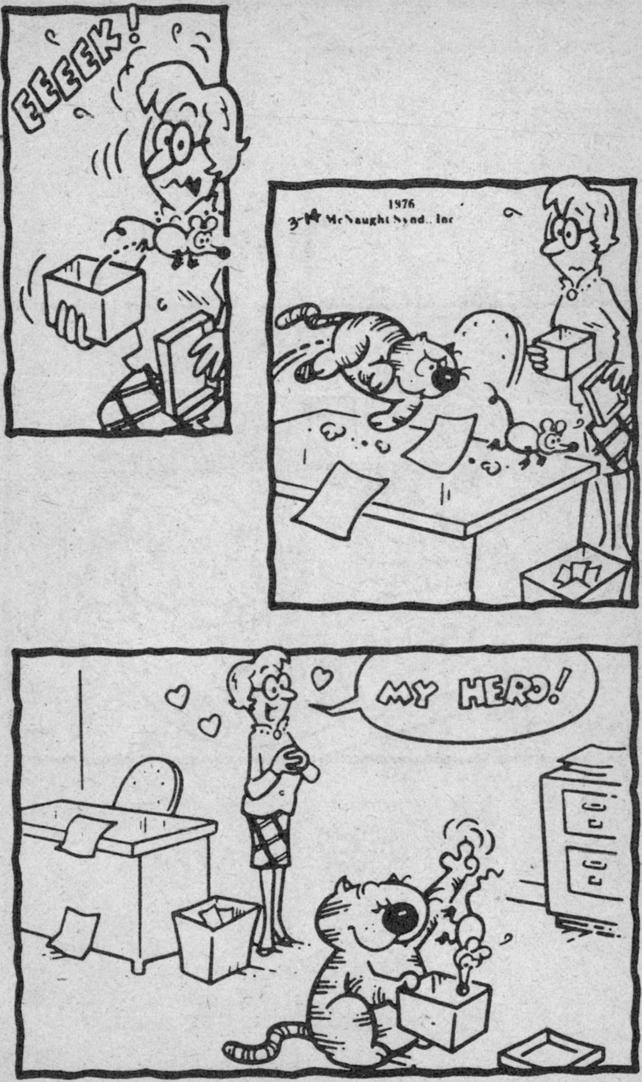
EEEEK!
1976
McNaught Synd., Inc
MY HERO!

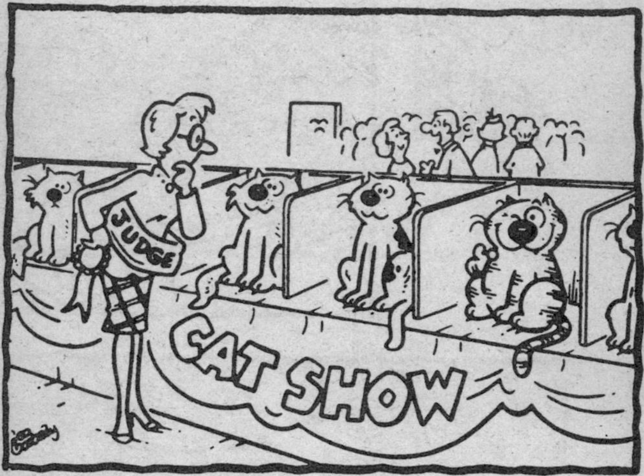
JUDGE
CAT SHOW

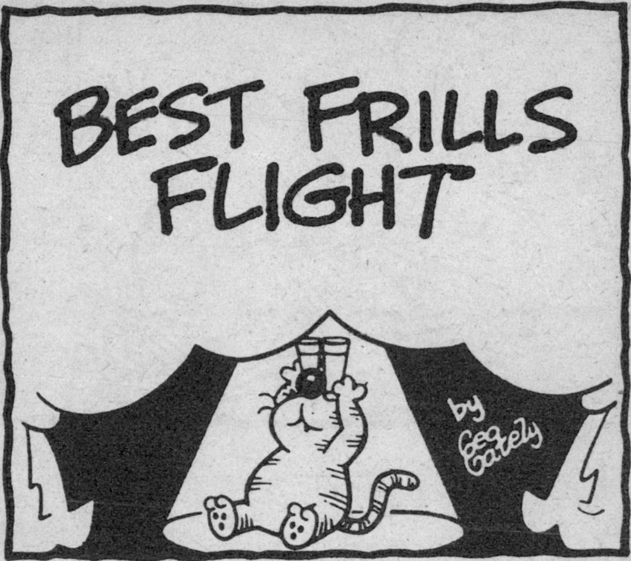
BEST FRILLS FLIGHT
by Geo Gately

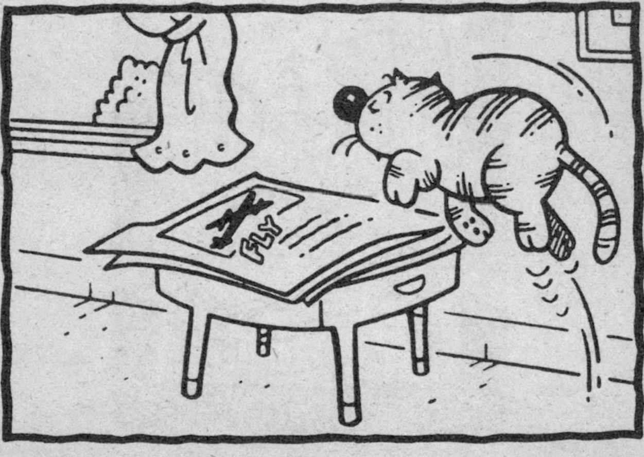
FLY

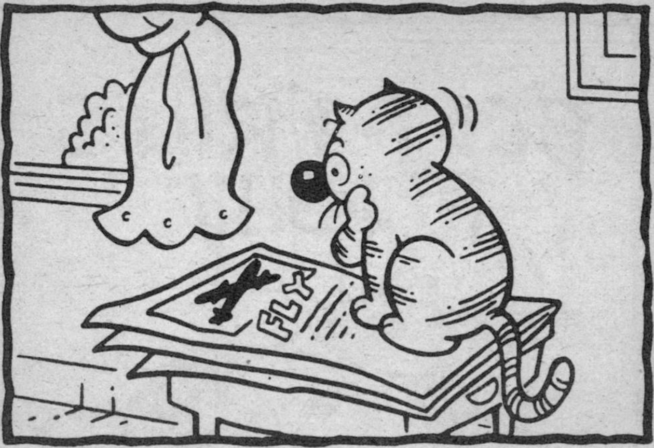
FLY

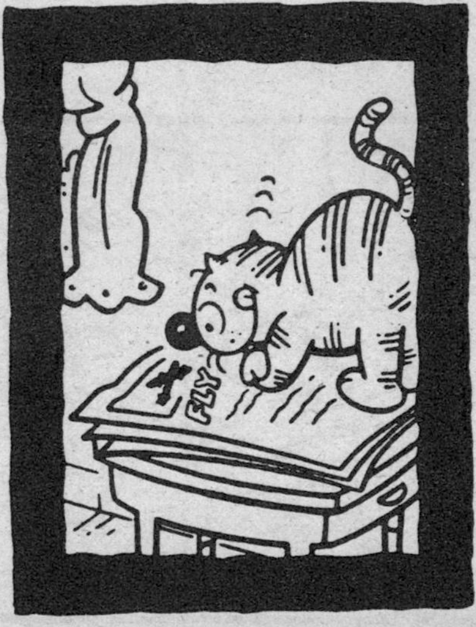
FLY

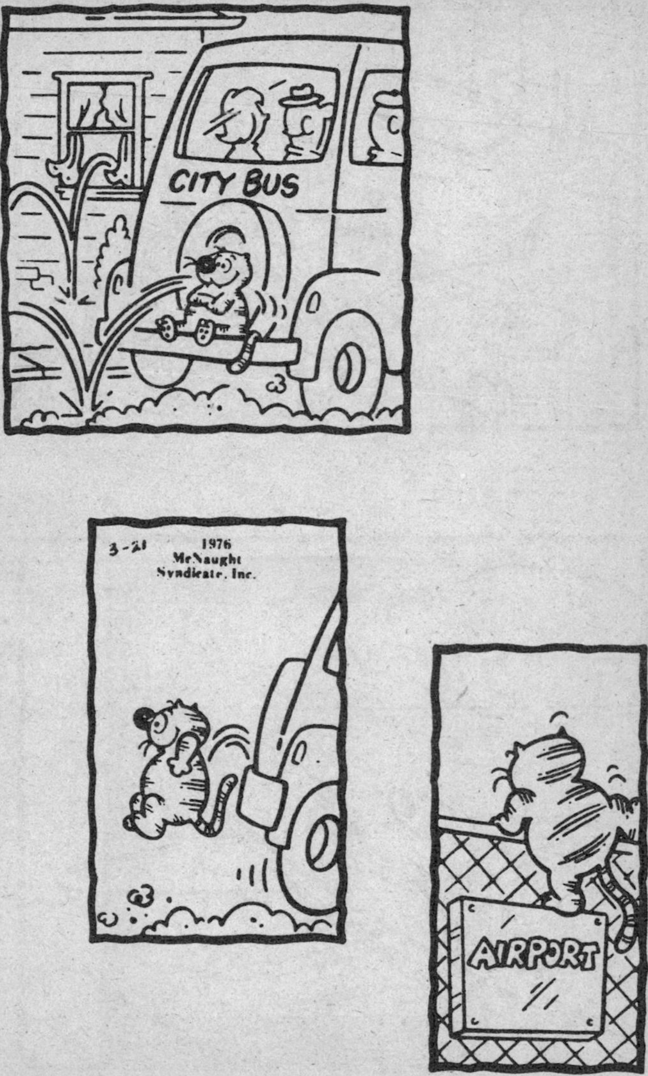
CITY BUS
3-21
1976
McNaught
Syndicate, Inc.
AIRPORT

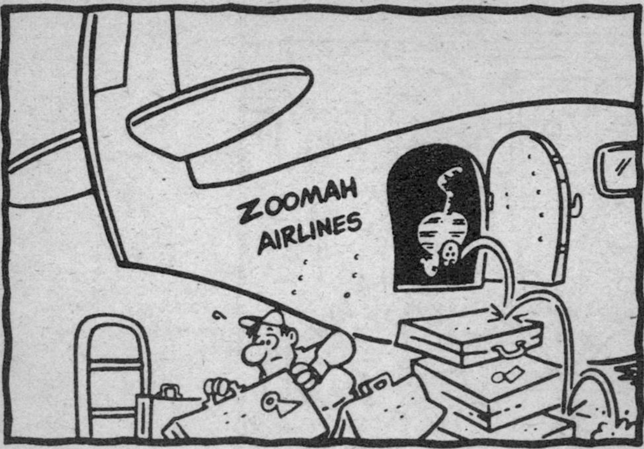
ZOOMAH
AIRLINES

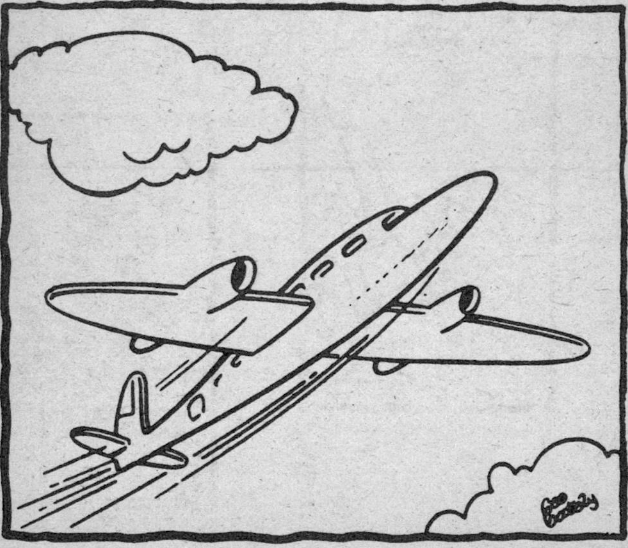

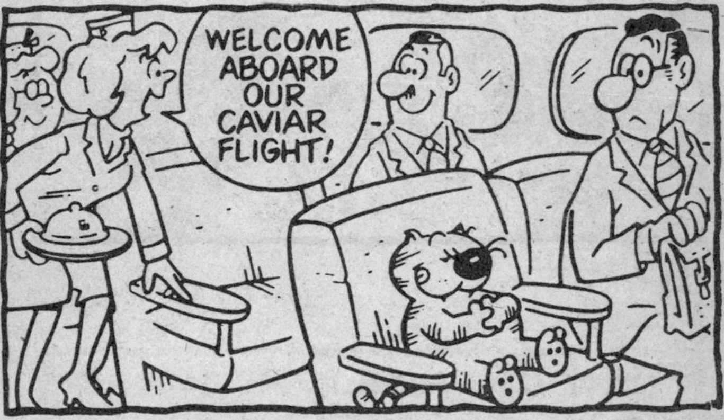
WELCOME ABOARD OUR CAVIAR FLIGHT!

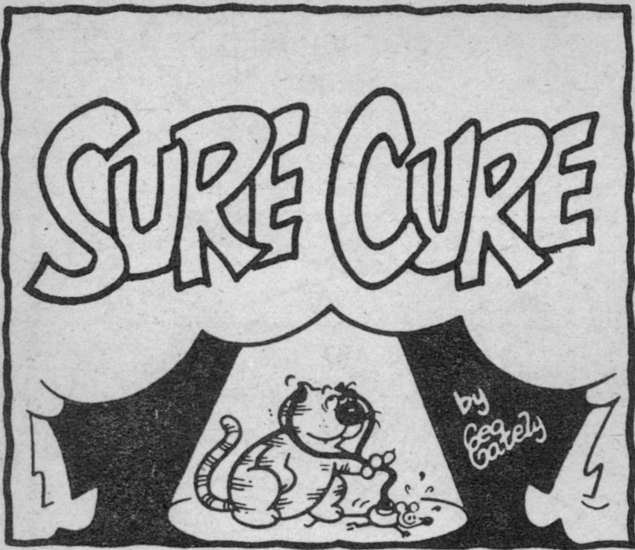
SURE CURE
by Geo Gately

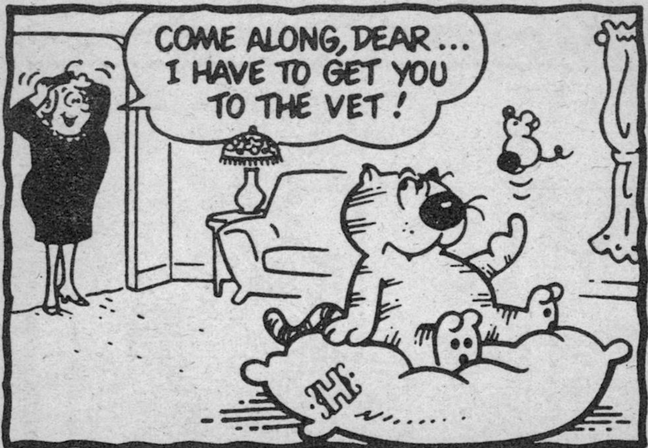
COME ALONG, DEAR... I HAVE TO GET YOU TO THE VET!

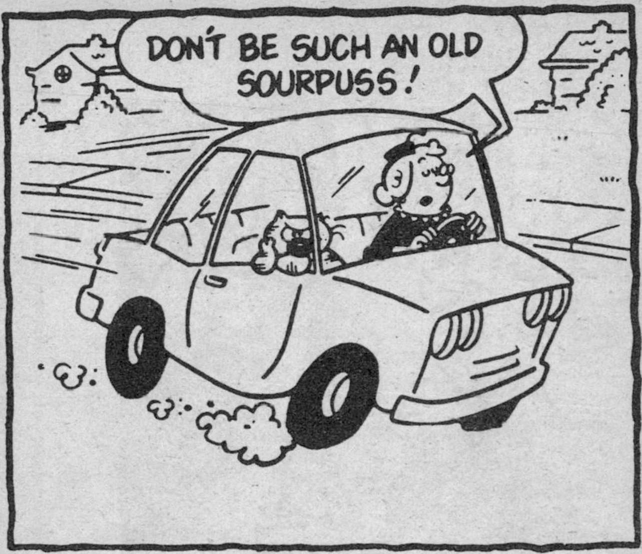
DON'T BE SUCH AN OLD SOURPUSS!

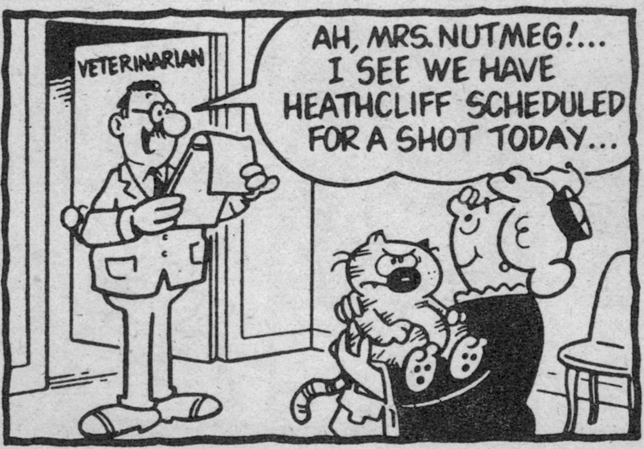
VETERINARIAN
AH, MRS. NUTMEG!... I SEE WE HAVE HEATHCLIFF SCHEDULED FOR A SHOT TODAY...

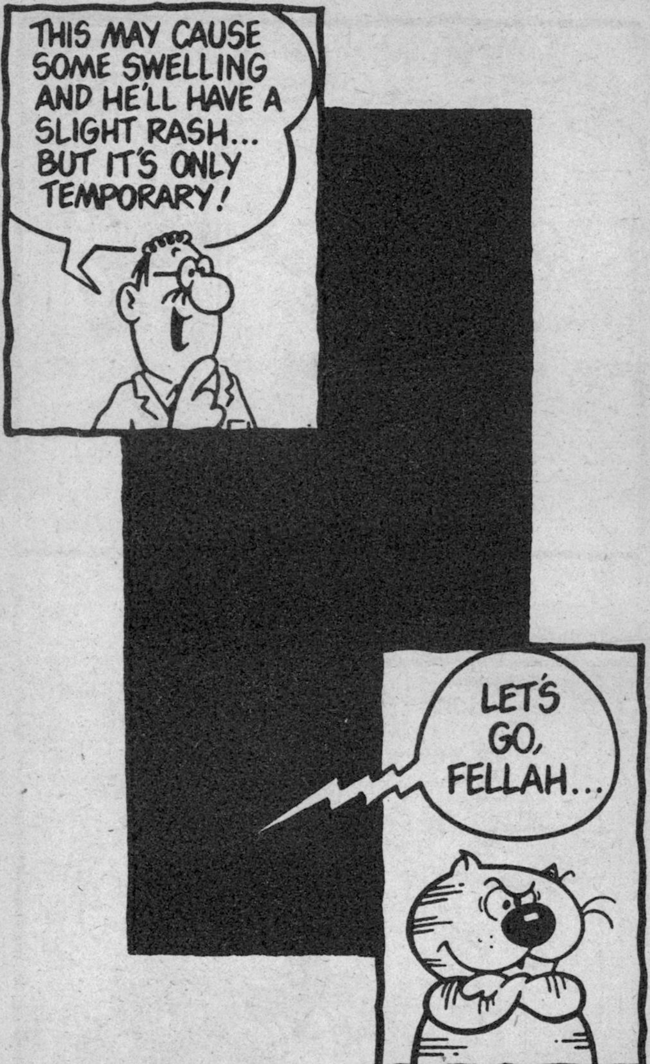
THIS MAY CAUSE SOME SWELLING AND HE'LL HAVE A SLIGHT RASH... BUT IT'S ONLY TEMPORARY!
LET'S GO, FELLAH...

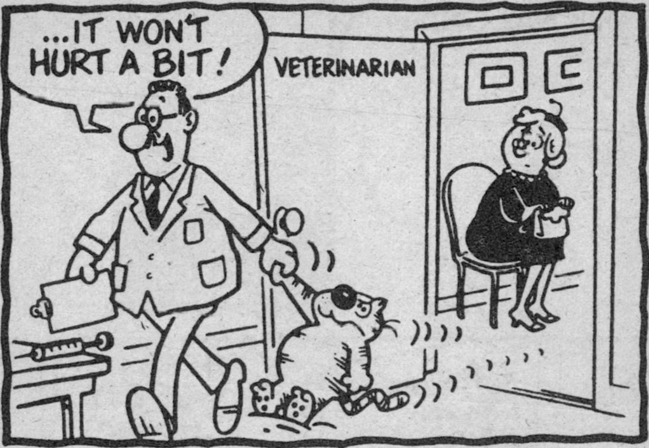
...IT WON'T HURT A BIT!
VETERINARIAN

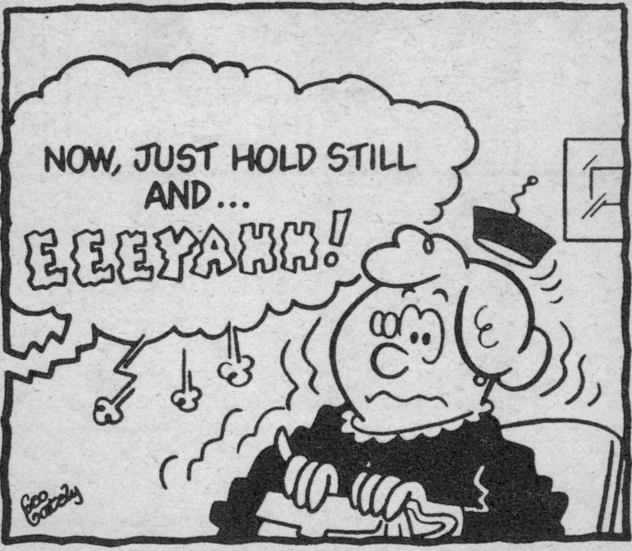
NOW, JUST HOLD STILL AND...
EEEYAHH!

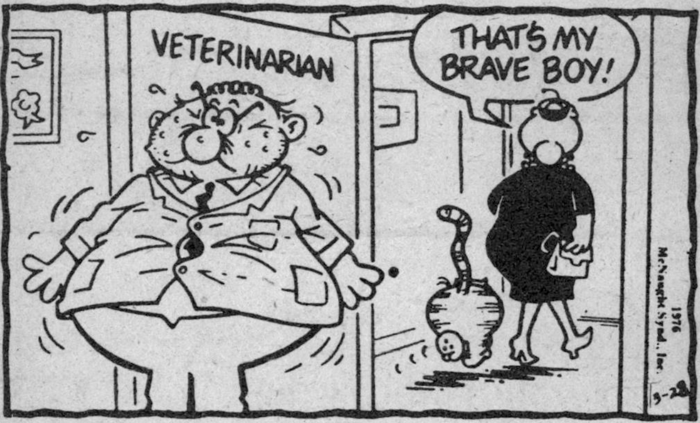
VETERINARIAN
THAT'S MY BRAVE BOY!
1976 McNaught Synd., Inc.

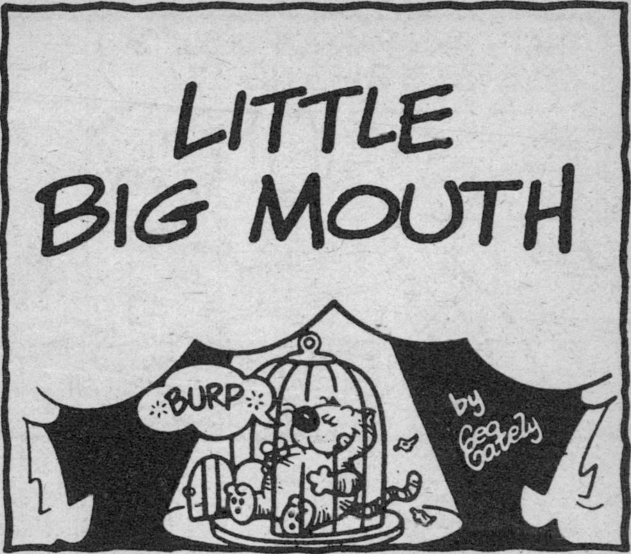
LITTLE
BIG MOUTH
BURP
by
Geo Gately

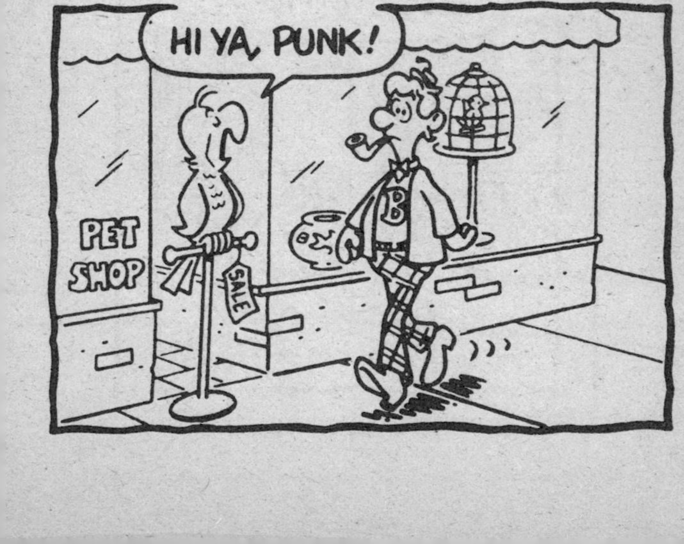
HI YA, PUNK!
PET
SHOP
SALE

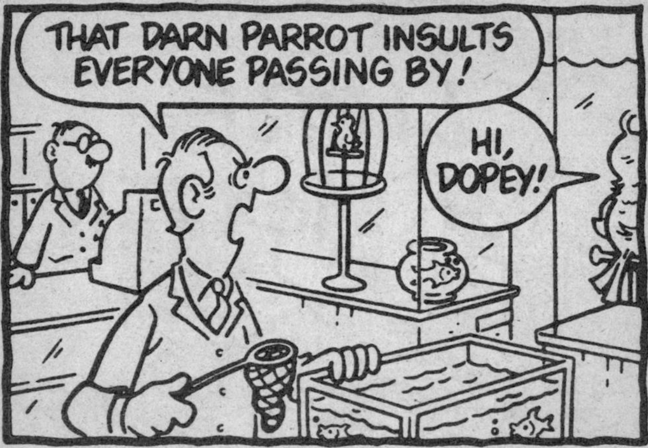
THAT DARN PARROT INSULTS EVERYONE PASSING BY!
HI, DOPEY!

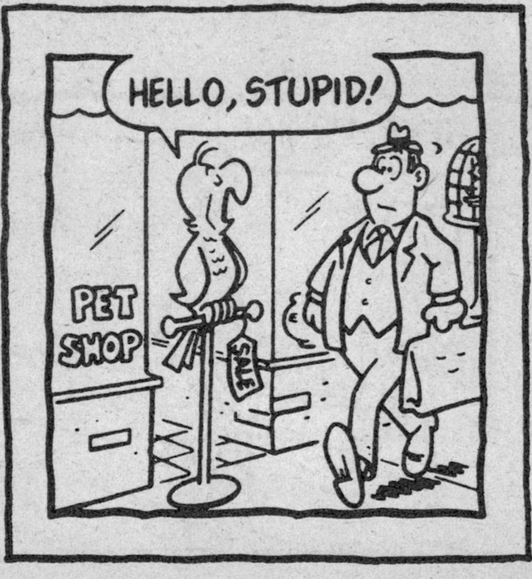
HELLO, STUPID!
PET SHOP
SALE

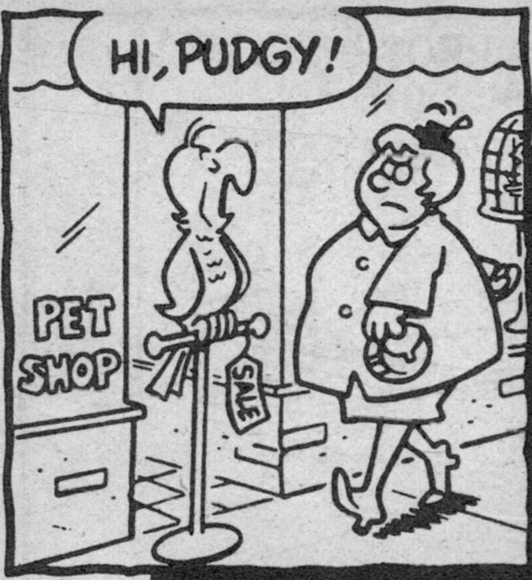
HI, PUDGY!
PET SHOP
SALE

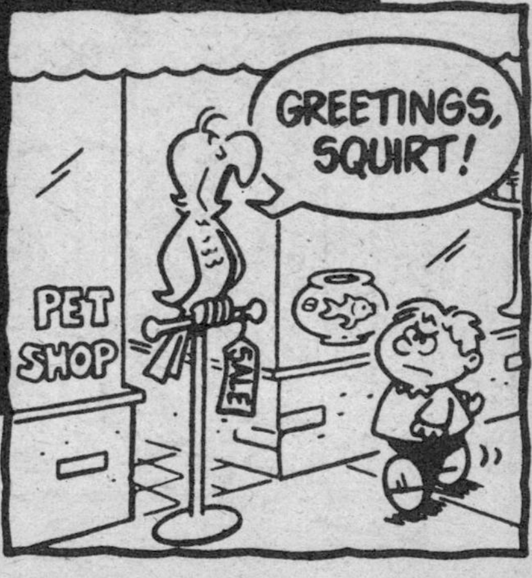
GREETINGS, SQUIRT!
PET SHOP
SALE

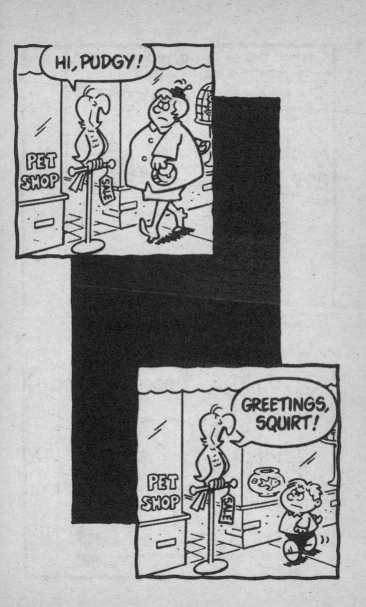

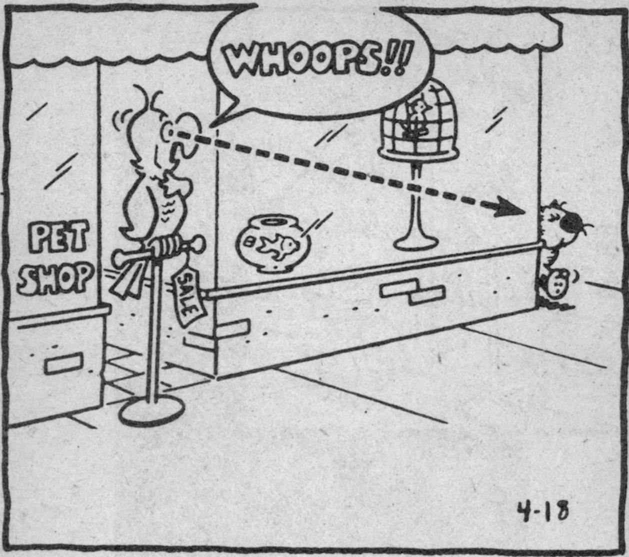
WHOOPS!!
PET SHOP
SALE
4-18

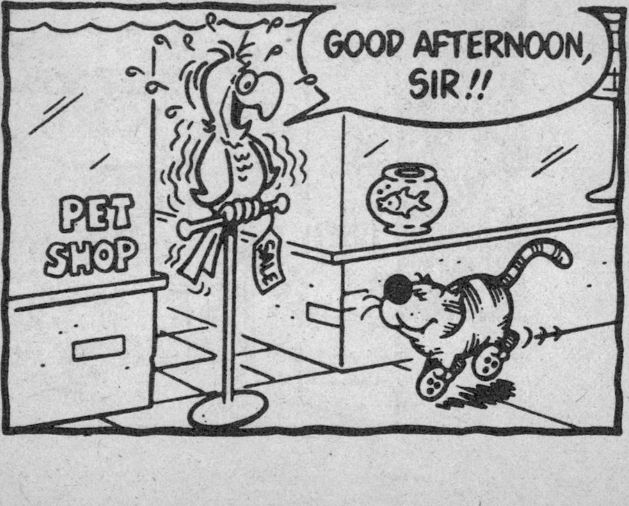
GOOD AFTERNOON, SIR!!
PET SHOP
SALE

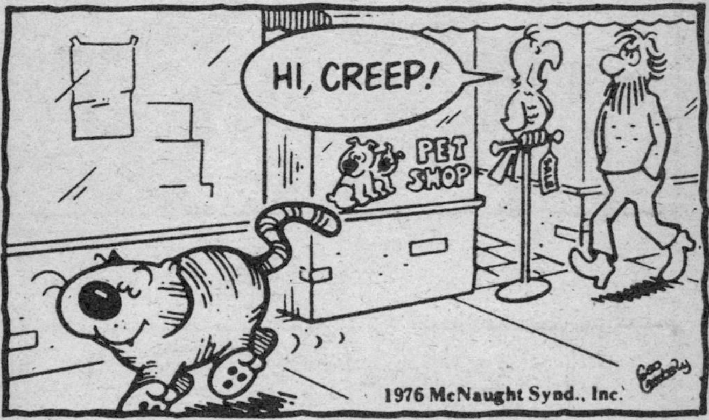
HI, CREEP!
PET SHOP
SALE
1976 McNaught Synd., Inc.

A DAY IN THE LIFE....
by Geo Gately

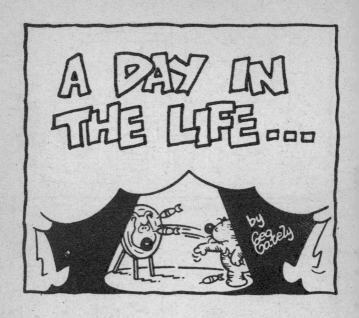

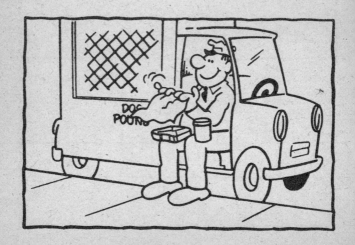

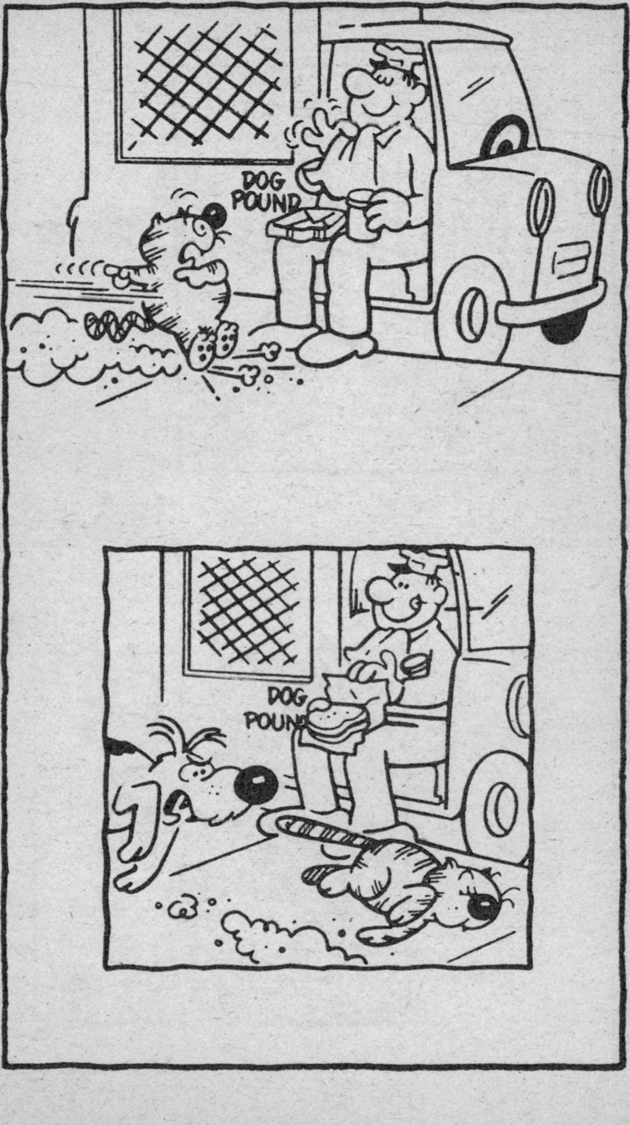
DOG POUND
DOG POUND

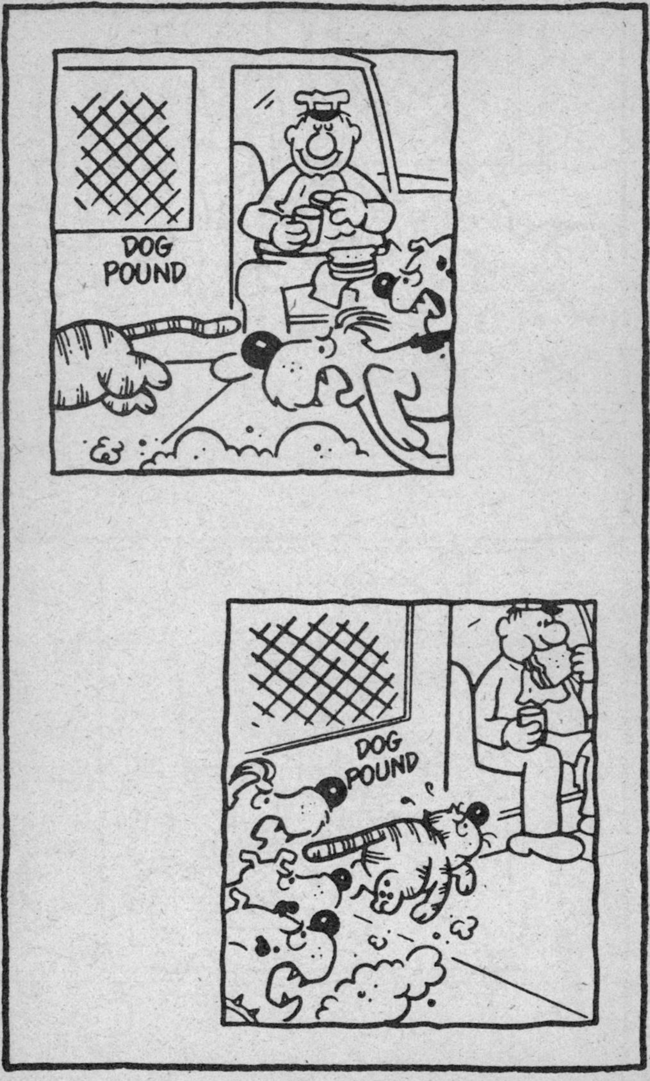
DOG POUND
DOG POUND

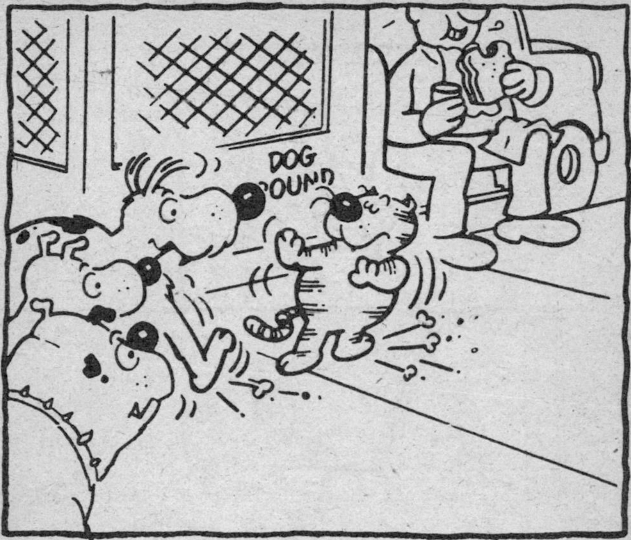
DOG
OUND

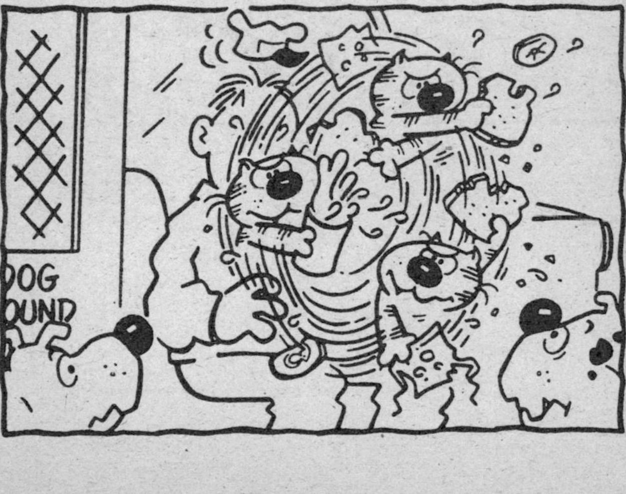
OOG
OUND

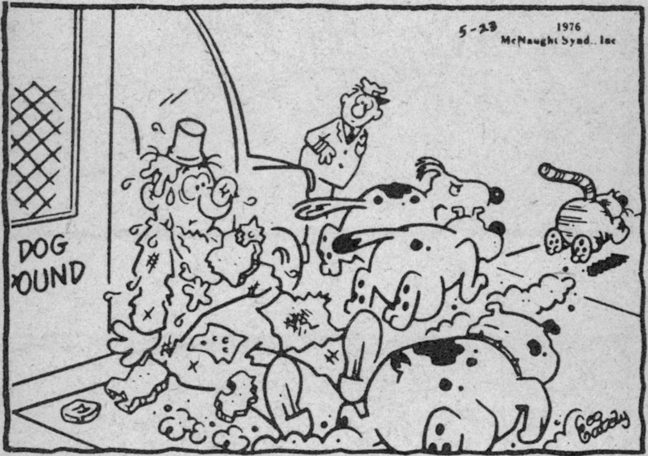
5-23
1976
McNaught Synd., Inc
DOG
OUND

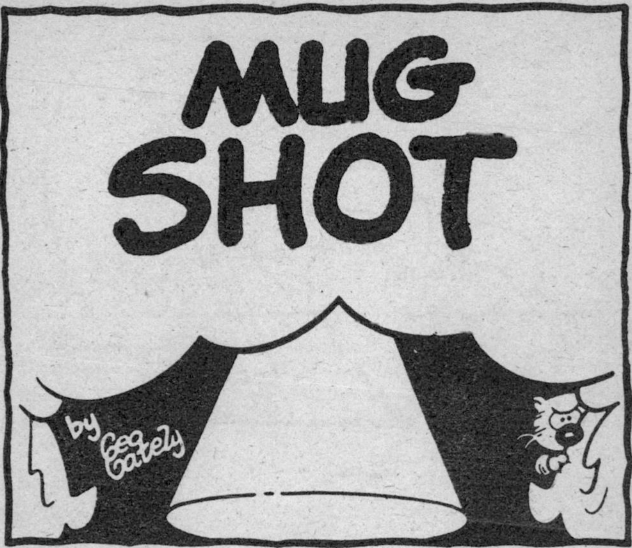
MUG
SHOT
by Geo Gately

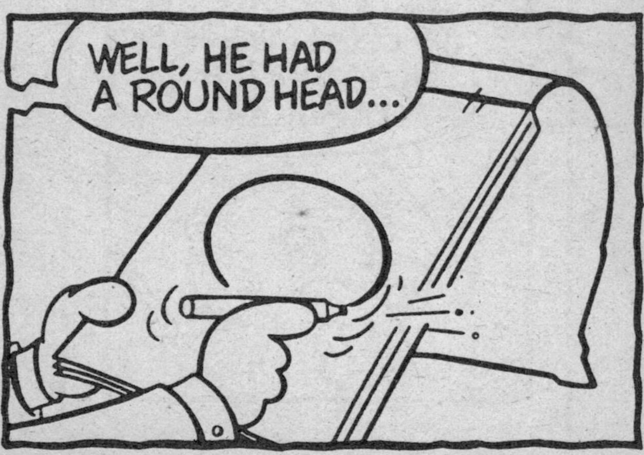
WELL, HE HAD A ROUND HEAD...

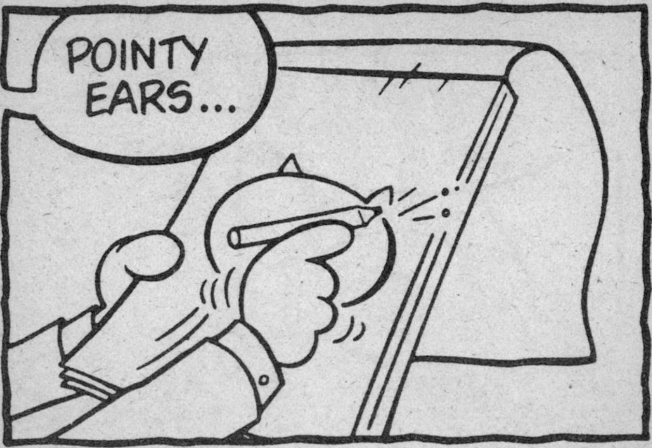
POINTY EARS...

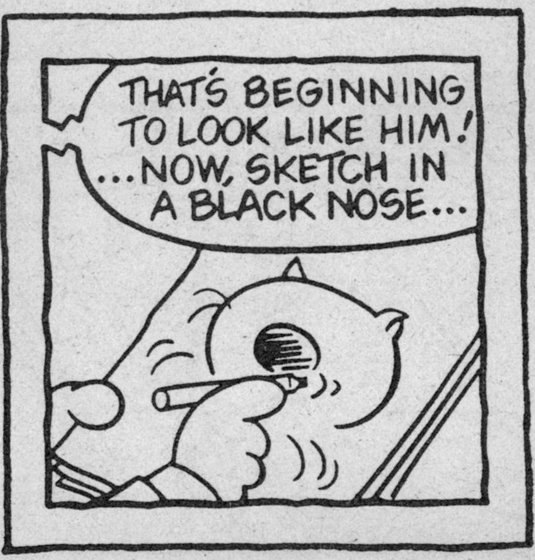
THAT'S BEGINNING TO LOOK LIKE HIM! ...NOW, SKETCH IN A BLACK NOSE...

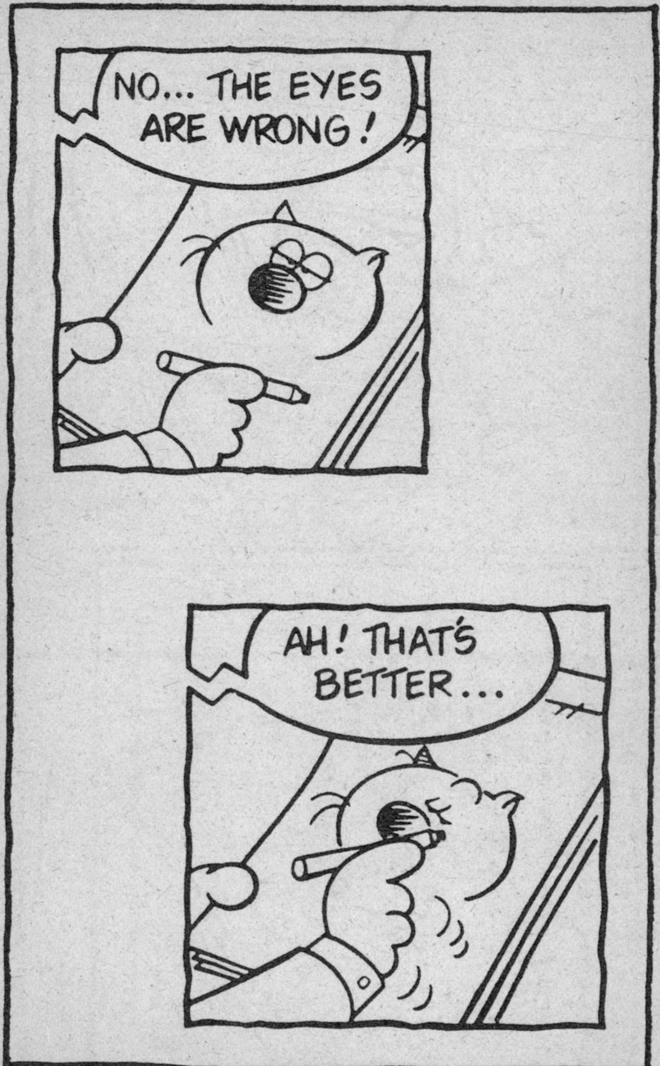
NO... THE EYES ARE WRONG!
AH! THAT'S BETTER...

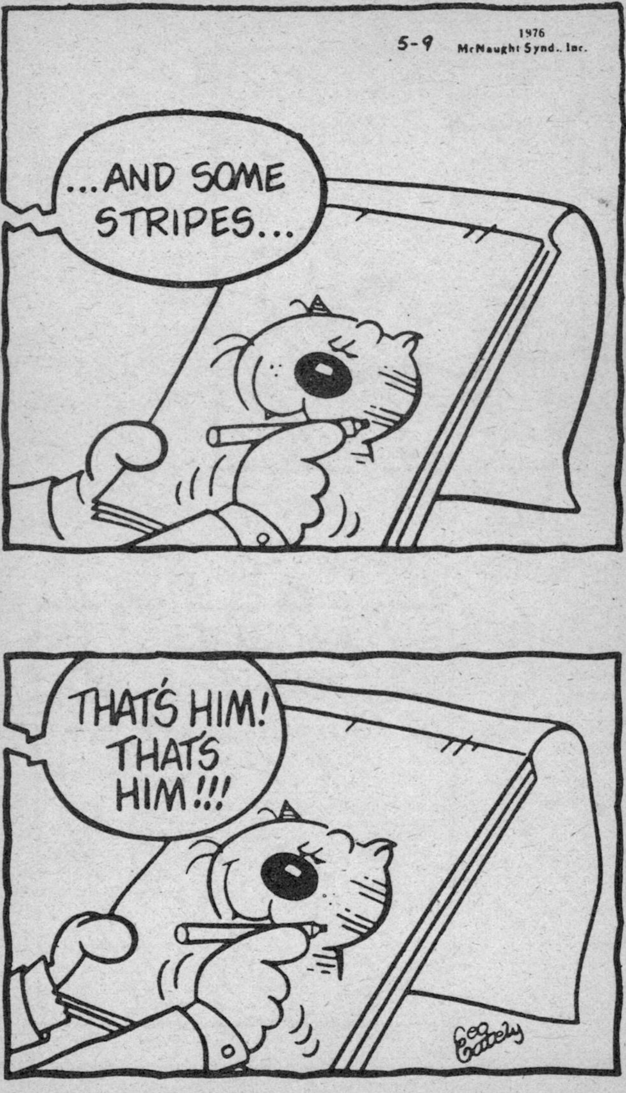
5-9
1976 McNaught Synd., Inc.
...AND SOME STRIPES...
THAT'S HIM! THAT'S HIM!!!

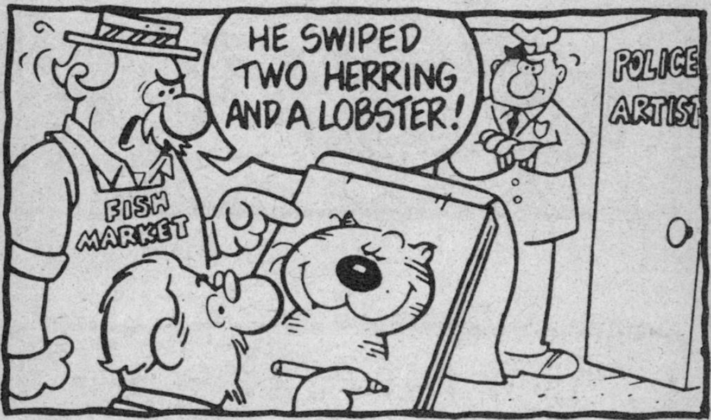
HE SWIPED TWO HERRING AND A LOBSTER!
FISH MARKET
POLICE ARTIST

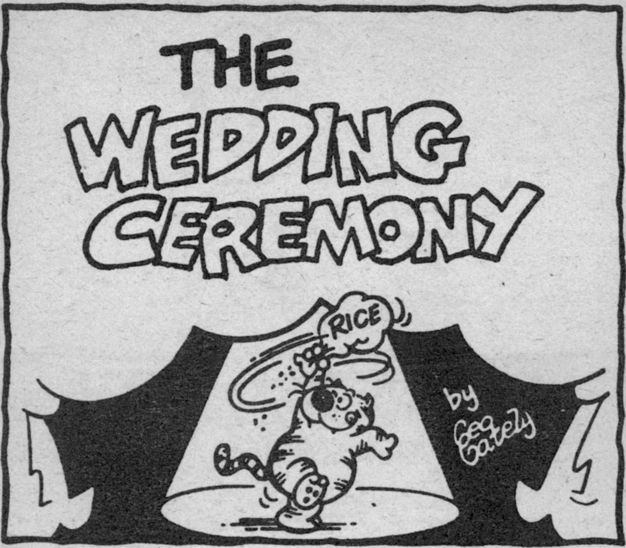
THE
WEDDING
CEREMONY
RICE
by
Geo Gately

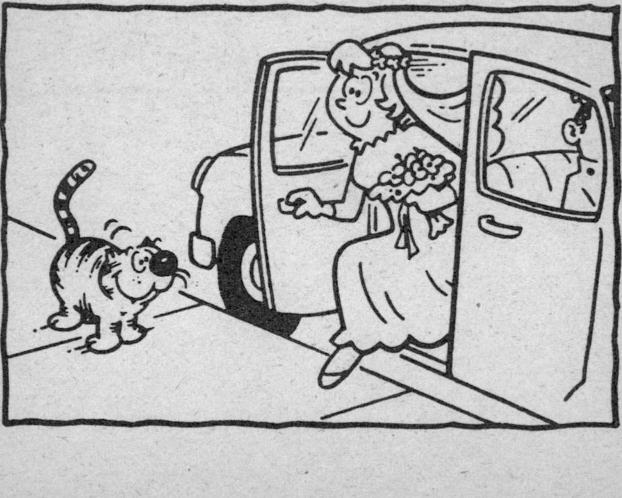

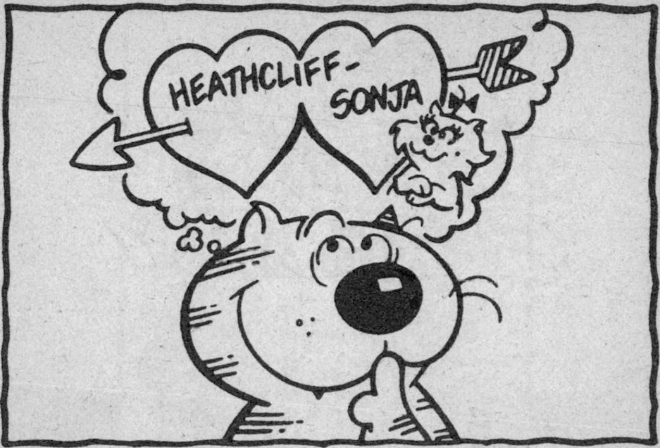
HEATHCLIFF-
SONJA

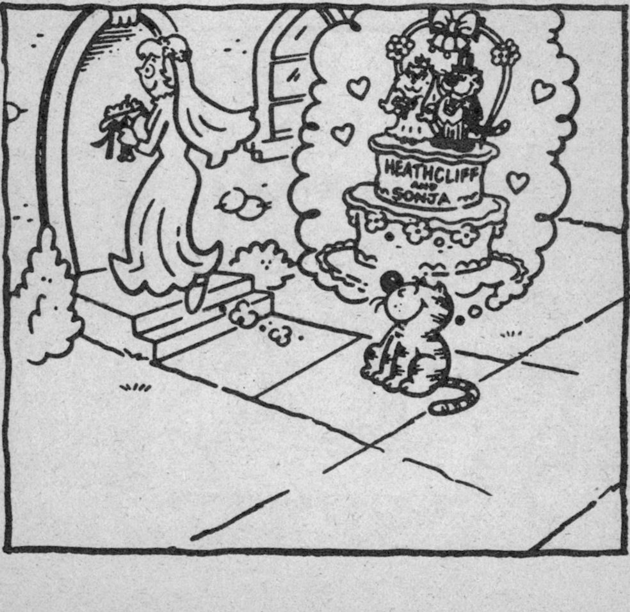
HEATHCLIFF AND SONJA

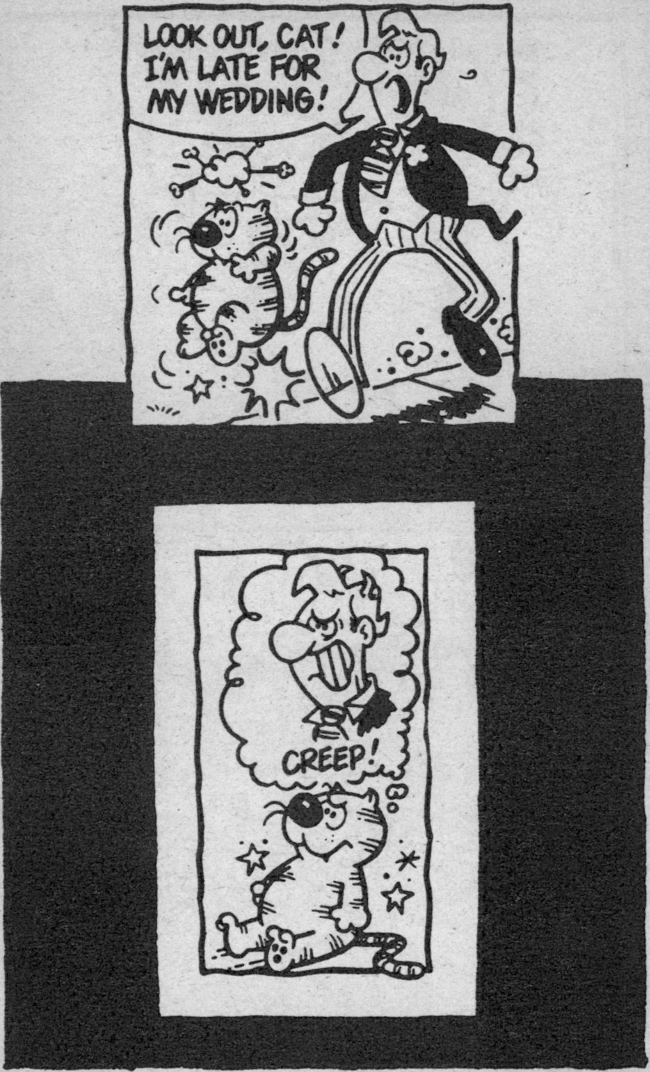
LOOK OUT, CAT! I'M LATE FOR MY WEDDING!
CREEP!

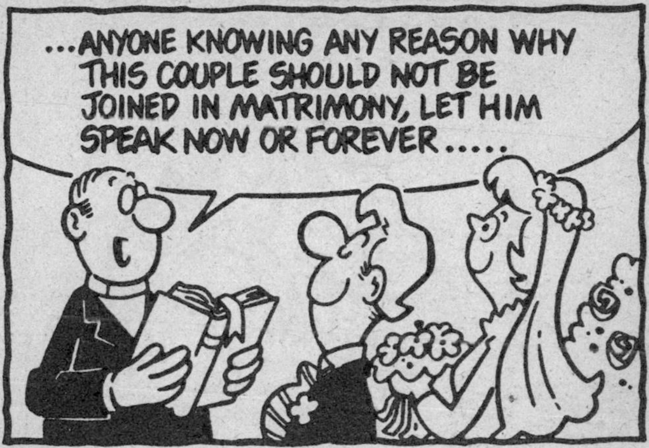
...ANYONE KNOWING ANY REASON WHY THIS COUPLE SHOULD NOT BE JOINED IN MATRIMONY, LET HIM SPEAK NOW OR FOREVER.....

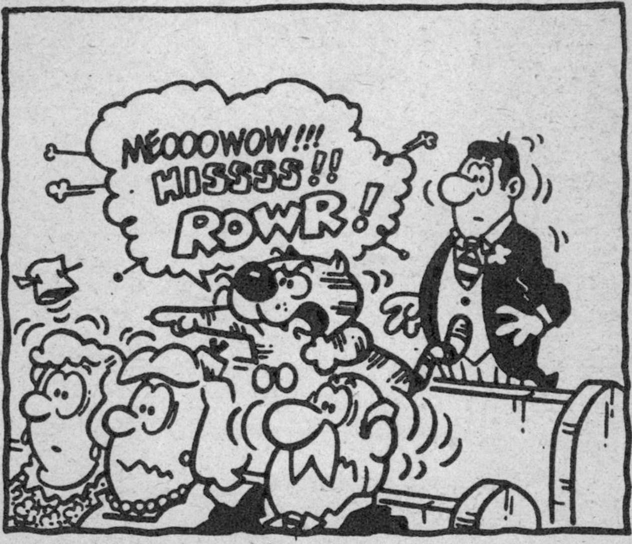
MEOOOWOW!!! HISSSS!! ROWR!

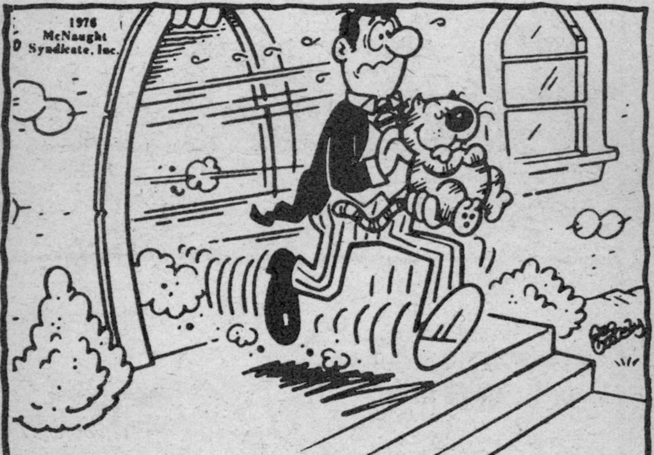

© 1976
McNaught
Syndicate, Inc.

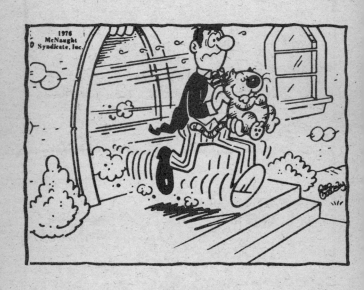

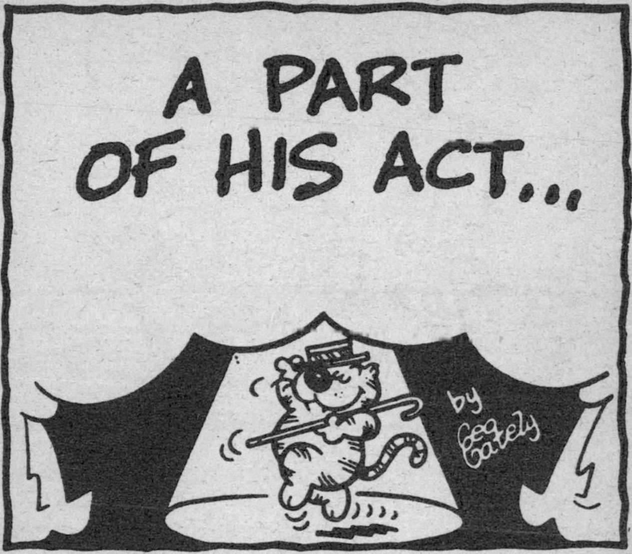
A PART OF HIS ACT...
by Geo Gately

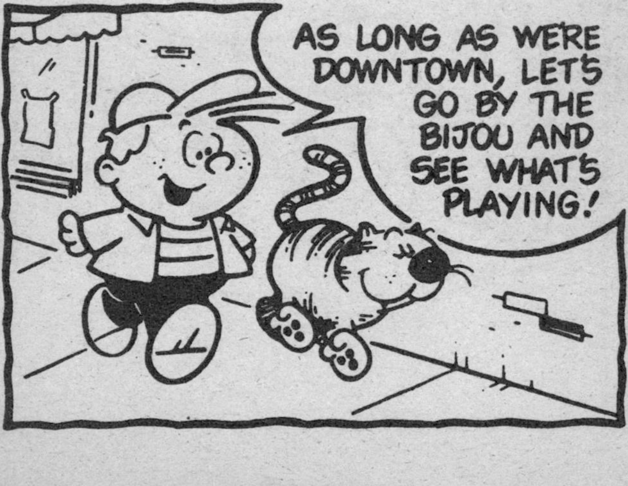
AS LONG AS WE'RE DOWNTOWN, LET'S GO BY THE BIJOU AND SEE WHAT'S PLAYING!

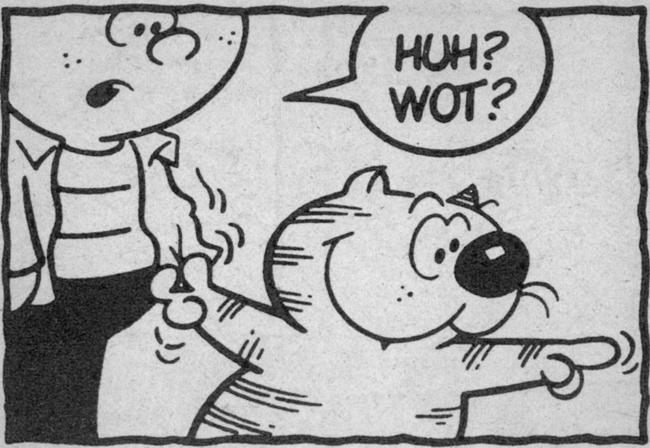
HUH?
WOT?

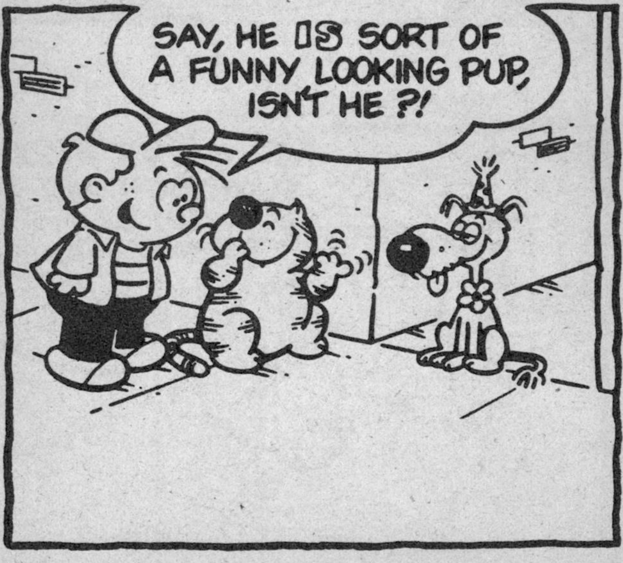
SAY, HE IS SORT OF A FUNNY LOOKING PUP, ISN'T HE ?!

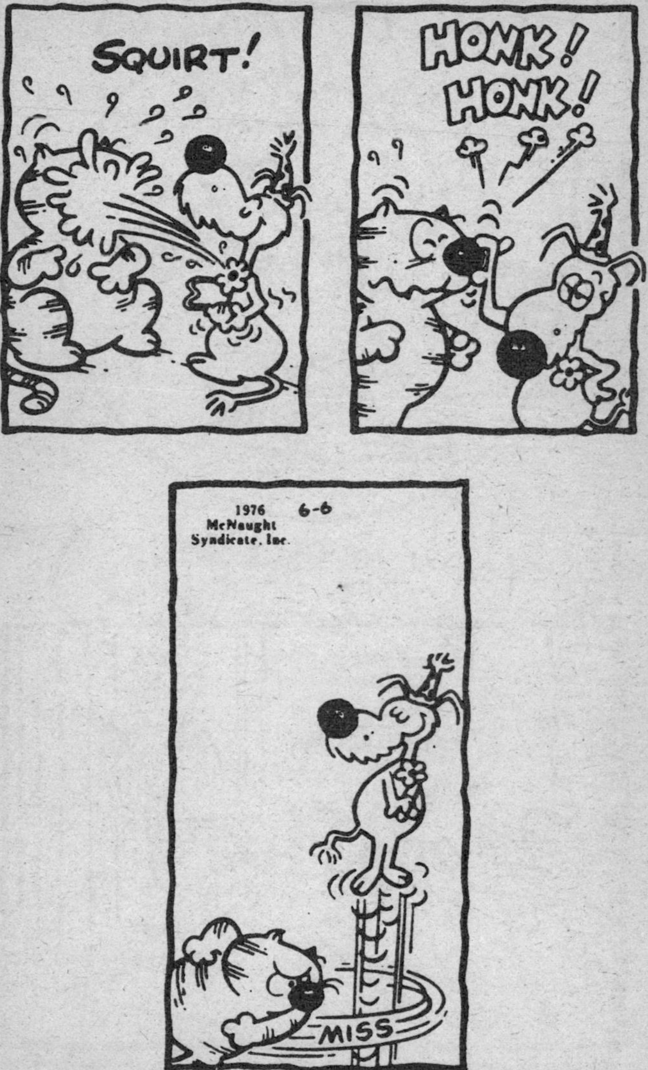
SQUIRT!
HONK! HONK!
1976 6-6
McNaught
Syndicate, Inc.
MISS

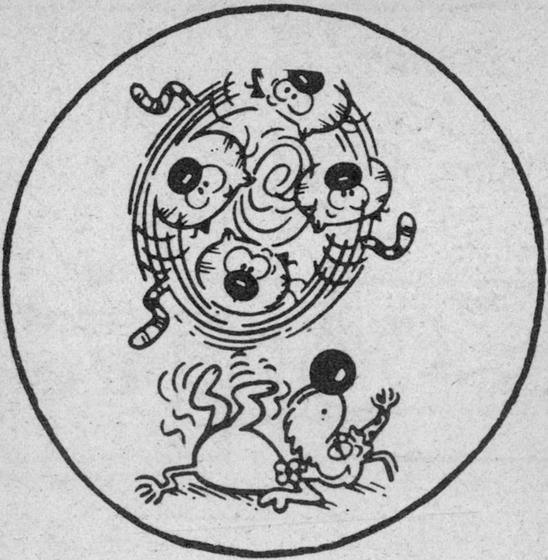

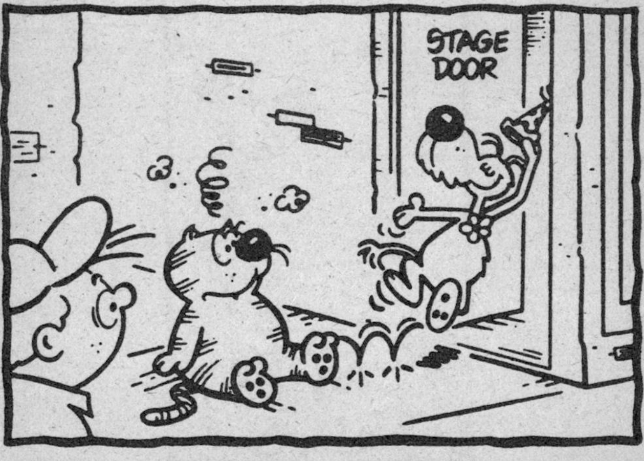
STAGE
DOOR

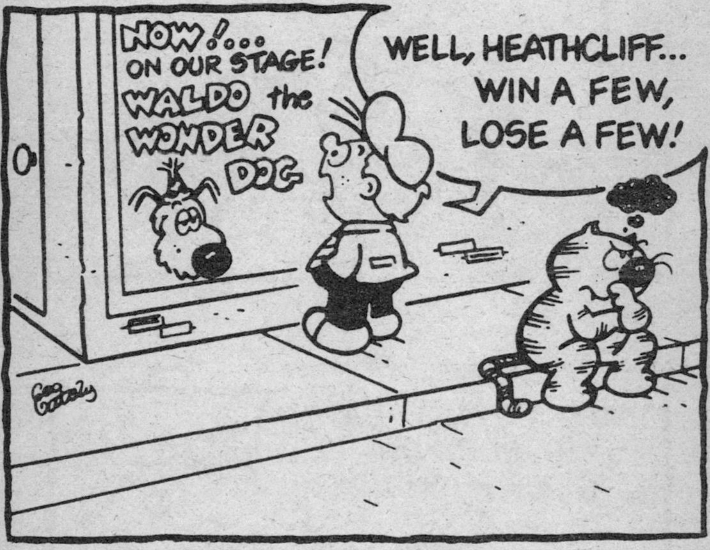
NOW!... ON OUR STAGE! WALDO the WONDER DOG
WELL, HEATHCLIFF... WIN A FEW, LOSE A FEW!

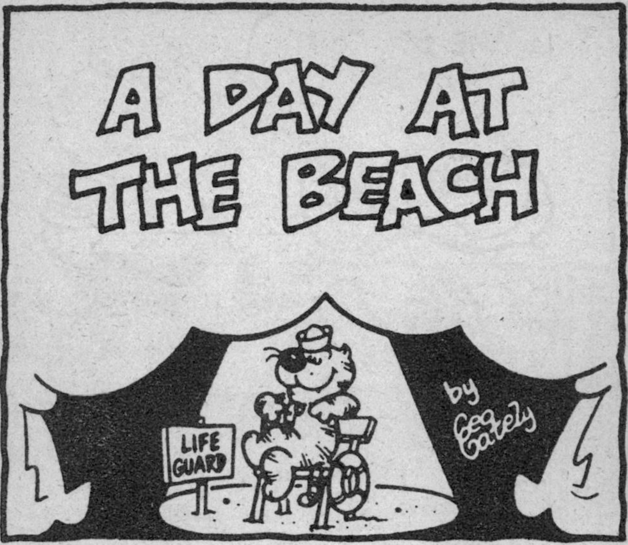
A DAY AT THE BEACH
LIFE GUARD
by
Geo Gately

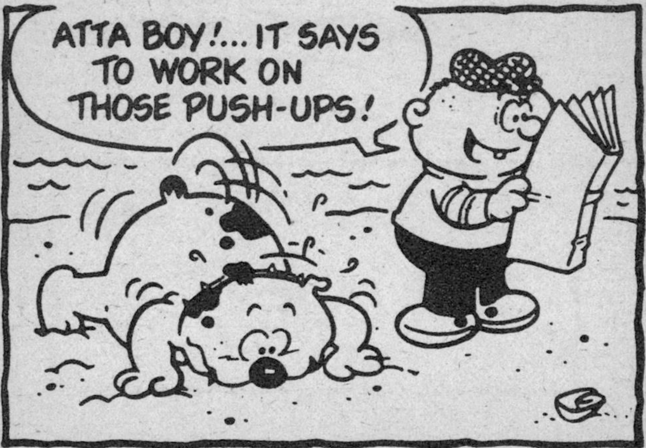
ATTA BOY!... IT SAYS TO WORK ON THOSE PUSH-UPS!

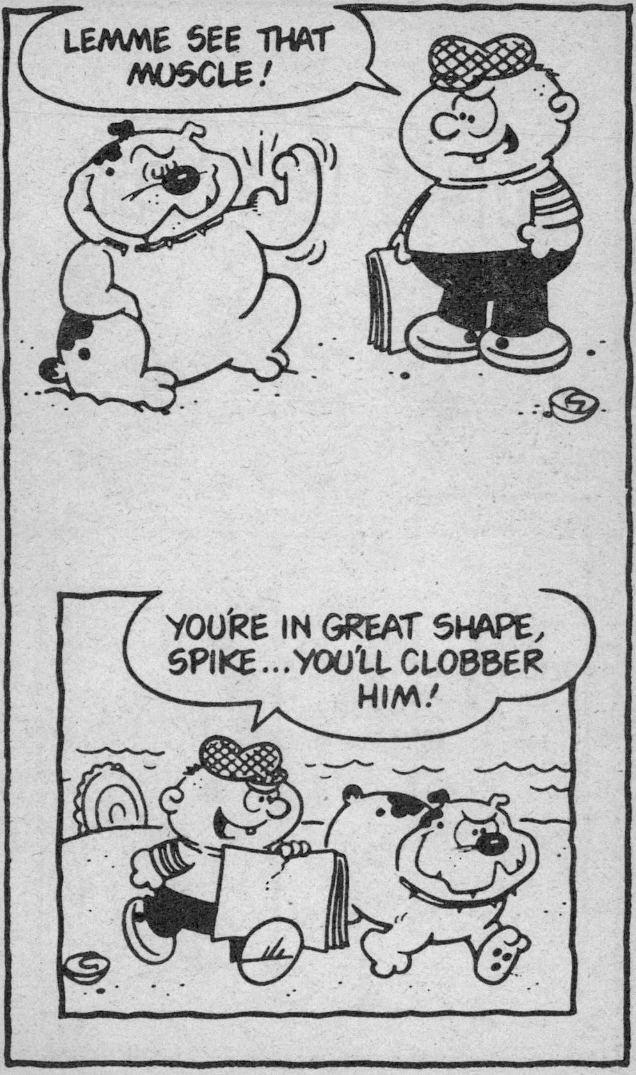
LEMME SEE THAT MUSCLE!
YOU'RE IN GREAT SHAPE, SPIKE... YOU'LL CLOBBER HIM!

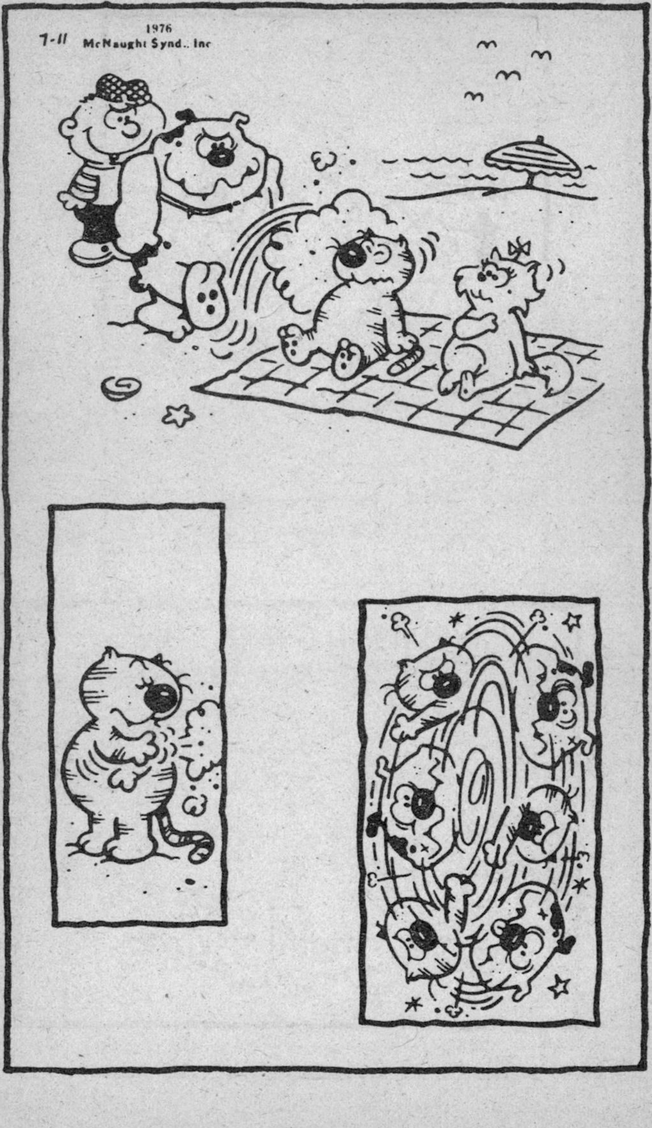
7-11
1976
McNaught Synd., Inc

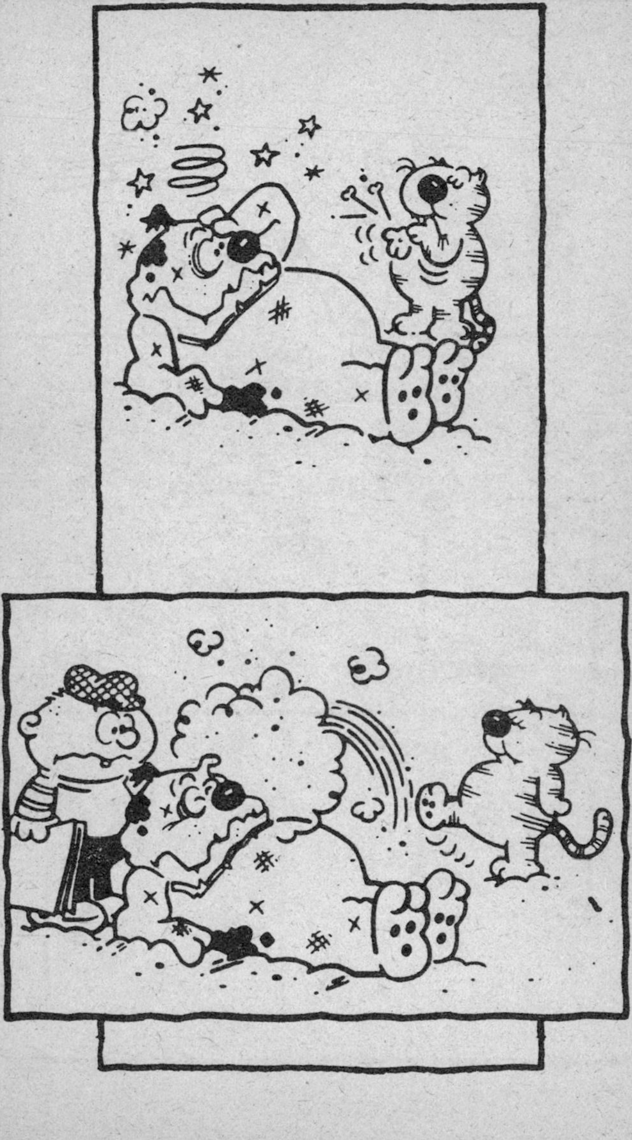

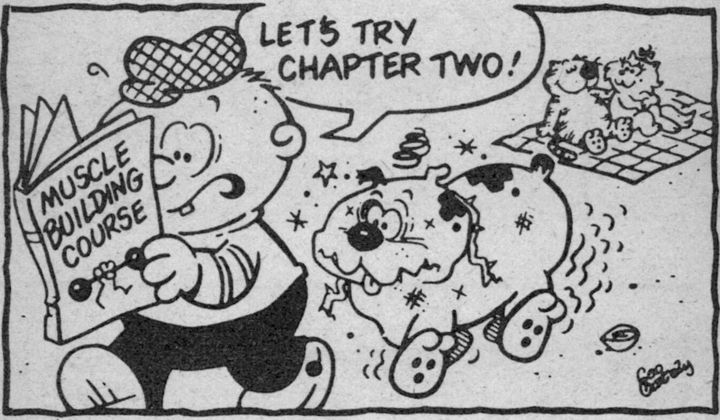
LET'S TRY CHAPTER TWO!
MUSCLE BUILDING COURSE

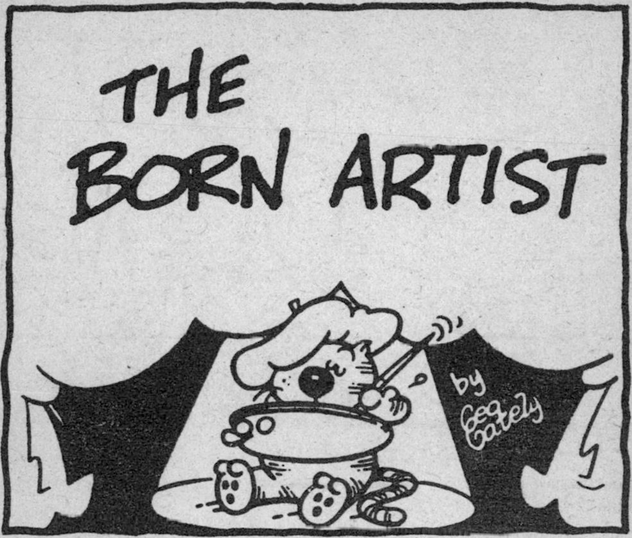
THE BORN ARTIST
by Geo Gately

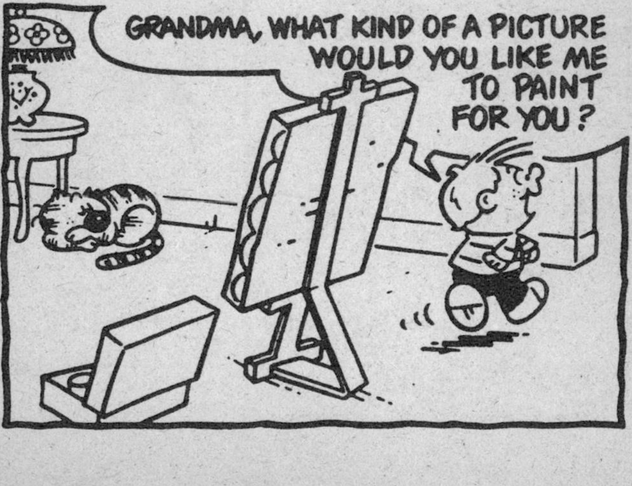
GRANDMA, WHAT KIND OF A PICTURE WOULD YOU LIKE ME TO PAINT FOR YOU?

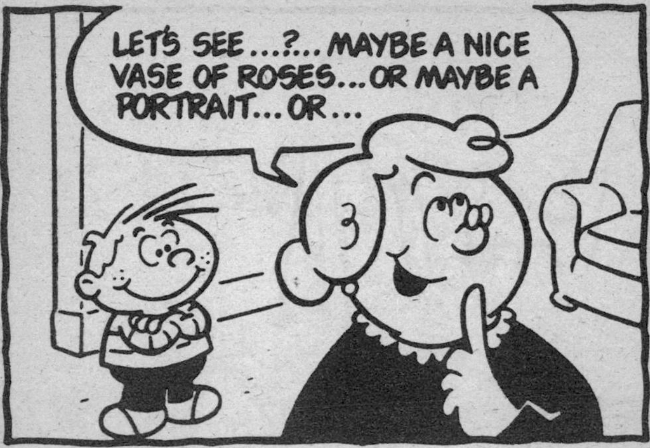
LET'S SEE ...?... MAYBE A NICE VASE OF ROSES... OR MAYBE A PORTRAIT... OR...

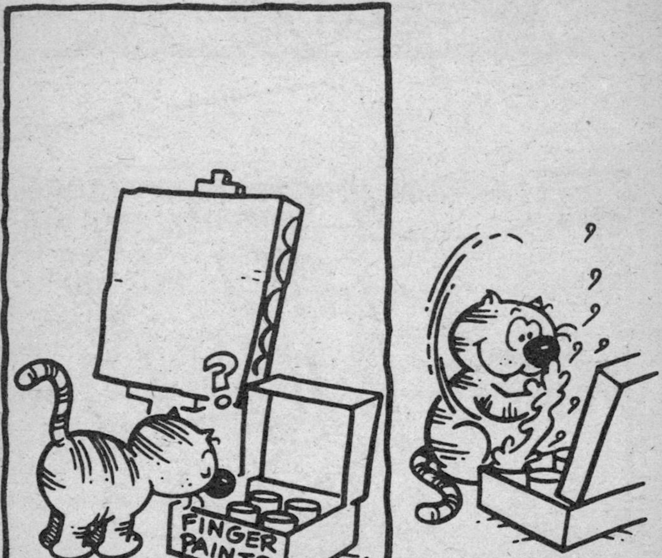
FINGER PAINTS

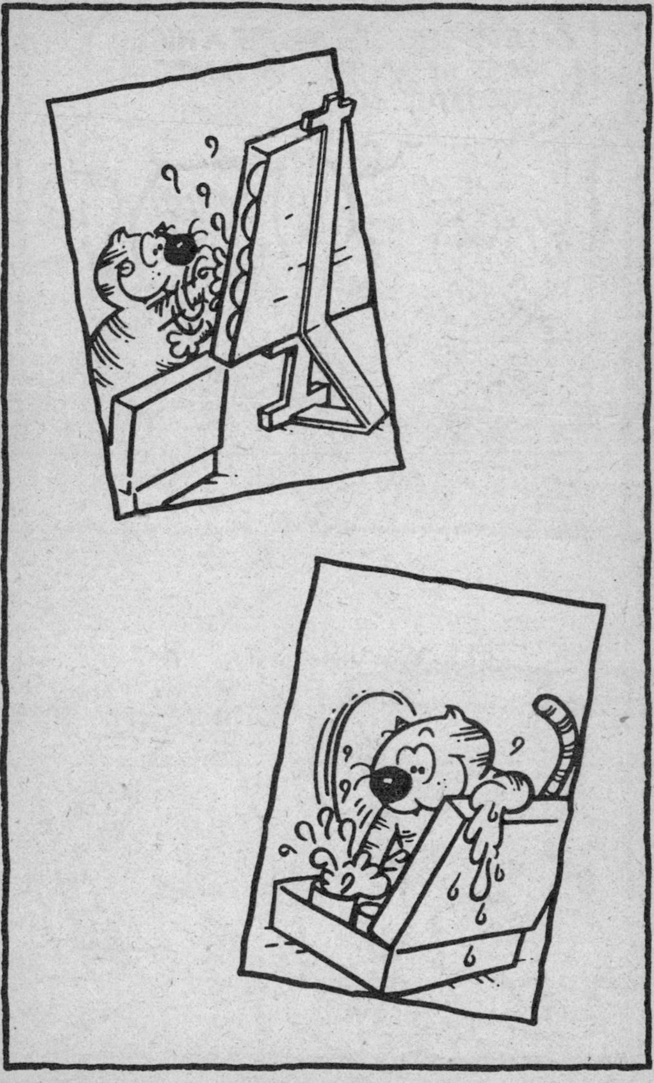

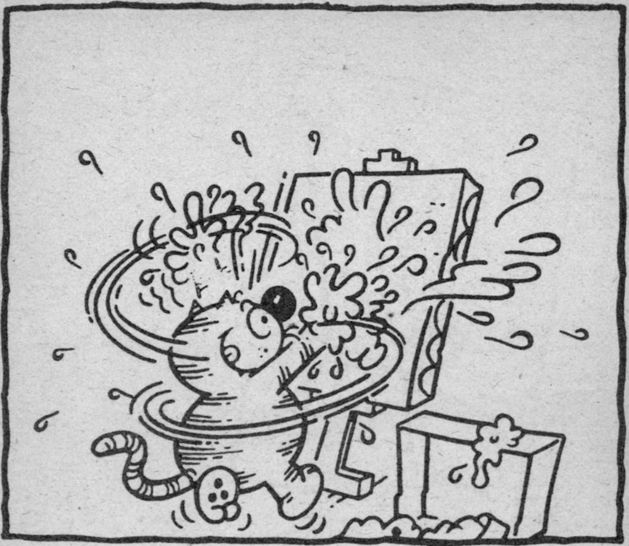

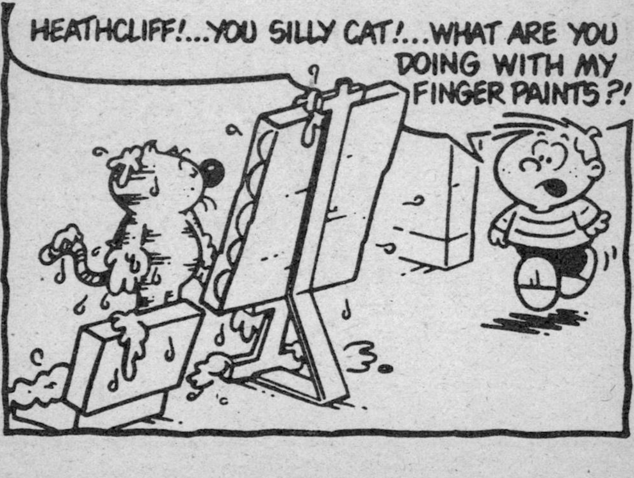
HEATHCLIFF!...YOU SILLY CAT!...WHAT ARE YOU DOING WITH MY FINGER PAINTS?!

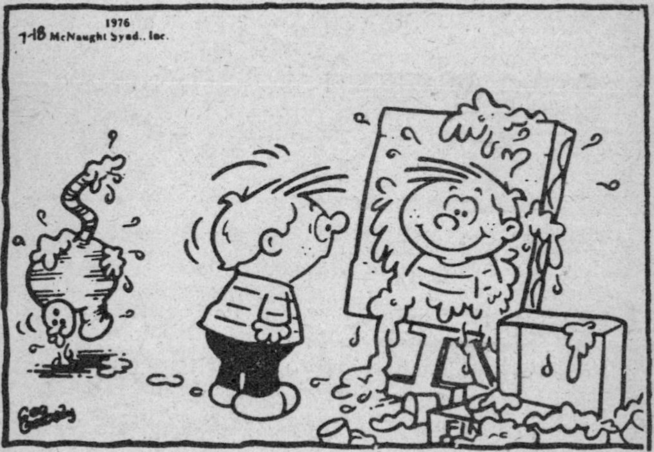
1976
7-18 McNaught Synd., Inc.

HEATHCLIFF

AMERICA'S CRAZIEST CAT

☐ 56800-1   SPECIALTIES ON THE HOUSE $1.95
    56801-X   Canada $2.50

☐ 56802-8   HEATHCLIFF AT HOME $1.95
    56803-6   Canada $2.50

☐ 56804-4   HEATHCLIFF AND THE $1.95
    56805-2   GOOD LIFE   Canada $2.50

☐ 56806-0   HEATHCLIFF: ONE, TWO, THREE $1.95
    56807-9   AND YOU'RE OUT   Canada $2.50

Buy them at your local bookstore or use this handy coupon:
Clip and mail this page with your order

TOR BOOKS—Reader Service Dept.
49 W. 24 Street, 9th Floor, New York, NY 10010

Please send me the book(s) I have checked above. I am
enclosing $_____ (please add $1.00 to cover postage
and handling). Send check or money order only—
no cash or C.O.D.'s.

Mr./Mrs./Miss _____

Address _____

City _____ State/Zip _____
Please allow six weeks for delivery. Prices subject to
change without notice.